THE CUCKOO IN SPRING

ELIZABETH CADELL

The Cuckoo in Spring

Queens House

FOREST HILLS, NEW YORK

Republished 1977 by Special Arrangement
with William Morrow Company

Copyright © 1954 by Elizabeth Cadell

*Fiction
Cad*

Library of Congress Cataloging in Publication Data
Cadell, Elizabeth.
  The cuckoo in spring.

  Reprint of the 1954 ed. published by Morrow, New York.
York.
  I. Title.
[PZ3.C11427Cu6]   [PR9499.3C3]   823'.9'12   77-8857
ISBN 0-89244-067-8

QUEENS HOUSE
P.O. Box 606
Forest Hills, New York 11375

Manufactured in the United States of America

With love to Hellin

THE CUCKOO IN SPRING

Chapter 1

MR. HURST, senior partner of the firm of Hurst & Son, Solicitors, sat at his office desk and stared moodily, and with a total lack of interest, at the pile of papers lying before him. He had been gazing at them for some time; nobody had disturbed him, for everyone in the office knew that he was feeling miserable, and everyone knew why; the old man, they said, was feeling like a fish out of water and would need time to get used to the new way of things.

The old order, and the new. Mr. Hurst, his fingers interlocked, his grey moustache drooping disconsolately, looked round at the new order and was engulfed by a wave of despair. This was what his son had decreed, and he was, his father felt bound to allow, a man of sound sense and clear vision. If he said that this was the kind of office Hurst & Son needed today, he was probably right. But for himself . . . Mr. Hurst sighed, adjusted his old-fashioned pince-nez on his nose and came to the decision which he now reached on an average of twice a day: he would go.

He would retire. His place had been in the old office in Chancery Lane, high, high up—four floors up—with a splendid vista of interesting rooftops and a fine view of the dome of St. Paul's. Up there, in five little rooms, back in the eighteen-thirties, the firm had been born. Up there in quarters confined but comfortable, shabby but snug, up there in the fusty-dusty atmosphere, with gas fires hissing and throwing rosy gleams over the rows of black boxes, each with a client's name printed upon it, up there he had worked and been happy—he and his father and his grandfather and great-grandfather before him. The place had suited him and he had suited the place. There was nothing for him here in these new premises, with a new desk and a new view and a new routine and a new stenographer. He had nothing specific against any of them; the view was as open as one could expect in this neighbourhood; the desk was expensive, the routine well-planned, the stenographer efficient. All the same, he was unhappy, and he felt out of his element. What was worse, he felt that he was not really needed. He had kept the business going and had brought his elder son into it; all that remained now was for him to step down and leave the young generation free to go on in the new ways. They could have their new site, decided Mr. Hurst bitterly; they could have their new office and their new staff. He had fought, at the beginning, a bloodless little battle to keep things as they were, and he had lost.

Mr. Hurst had suffered a great many domestic defeats in his time. As he sat at his shining, too-tidy desk, he looked back without rancour at some of them. He had wanted a large family—round dozen or so, but he had been brought up short with two sons and a daughter. He had wanted a William and a George and a Mary and he had found himself with an Oliver and a Julian and a Drusilla. He had put their names down at one set of schools and had found himself paying the fees of another. He had wanted both sons in the business and had got only one—and one of them, remembered Mr. Hurst, coming back to the present, was enough; one of them had revolutionized it and turned it, in less than six years, from what it had been into what it was now; from an old-fashioned family business into an up-to-date and impersonal one. A whole first floor instead of half a fifth floor; an office bright and open instead of cozy and dark and intimate. Gone were the little rooms and the familiar clutter of this and that, with dear, old, old-established Miss Sterndale sitting by him, facing him, instead of new young Miss What's-her-name at a desk against the window, sitting with her back turned to him and blocking what there was in the way of view. It was all very smart and new and bleak and unfriendly, and he had no part in it and it was time he went. He had been in the firm . . . Mr. Hurst took up a pencil and made a calculation on his blotting pad. He had joined at seventeen, without the university education which both his sons had enjoyed. Seventeen from let-me-see, seven from three leaves . . . borrow one . . . that came to—no! That was obviously incorrect. He'd made an error somewhere, added up the tens twice. Three from . . . but it was not incorrect. It was right. It was . . . Good God! Forty-four years! Forty-four years! Day in, day out, week by week and year by year—forty-four years! If you added seventeen to forty-four . . . Mr. Hurst added it, put down his pencil and stared with glazed and unseeing eyes at the neat back of his stenographer. Where had it gone? How had it gone? Old! He was an old

3

man and he ought to have got out years ago instead of sitting here in his dotage, trying to make up his mind to leave. Leave? Why, of course he'd leave. He'd speak to Oliver about it today; this morning; now, in fact. He'd go and look for him behind that glass partition at the other end of the office and get the thing over and done with.

Mr. Hurst, preparing to rise and storm the glass partition, found his own door opening, and looked up to see his son entering the room. He leaned back in his chair and, studying him with a new detachment, saw that this was no boy; this was a man of thirty, tall, well-built, with steady eyes and a firm jaw and—already—the look of a successful man of business.

" 'Morning, Father." Oliver's voice matched his appearance —it was pleasant, steady, and had the least touch of gravity. "I'd like to have a word with you about Mr. Randall."

Brief and to the point, completely business-like, noted old Mr. Hurst. When he had married and gone to live in a house of his own, as Oliver had done, his morning greeting to his father, when they met in the office, had always begun on a family note. "Good morning, Father; how's Mother today?" he would say. "How's the new cook doing? Good. Thought I'd look in tonight with Judith and sample the cooking." But there were no family touches nowadays. Good morning . . . and to business.

Oliver, glancing at his father, recognized the signs. The old man was feeling moody. He was homesick; he missed the old premises at the top of a rickety building, with no elevator, and stairs so dark and so dangerous that elderly clients—and most of the clients had passed the seventy mark— who got to the top without breaking their necks, had had to re- sort to their heart tablets before being able to state the object

4

of their visit. A crow's nest, but with nothing airy about it; musty and dusty and out of date. The move to new premises had been long overdue, but it was hard on the old man.

"What about Randall?" asked the old man. "Oh—the pictures."

"Yes." Oliver sat on a corner of the big desk and lit a cigarette. "I suppose you didn't mention it to Julian?"

At the mention of his younger son, Mr. Hurst's moustache drooped more hopelessly than ever. There had never been a Julian Hurst before—and there had never been a Hurst like Julian.

The Hursts, as Mr. Hurst himself had pointed out to his wife when he proposed to her, were a dull lot. Worthy, sober, hard-working and thrifty—they were all this, but they laid no claim to lighter qualities, and his surprise at falling in love with a humourous and light-hearted girl had been equalled only by his astonishment at learning that she returned his affection. The marriage had been a happy one, but in his children Mr. Hurst detected characteristics which the Hursts had never had before and which, in his more despondent moments, he felt that they had done very well without. In Oliver he sometimes saw, with relief, a touch of his own soberness, but in Julian and Drusilla there was no sign of anything of the kind.

Julian had refused outright to go into his father's firm. A talented artist, he had at first planned to make money by selling his pictures, and Mr. Hurst, though distrusting anything that his younger son embarked upon, had found it difficult to take a firm line, for all three of his children had, at the age of twenty-one, come into an inheritance which provided them with adequate incomes of their own. But after two years of trying, unsuccessfully, to sell his own pic-

5

tures, Julian had discovered that he could make a better living by selling other people's. He had opened an art shop in Kensington, in partnership with his mother's sister, Mrs. Rowena Aintree, and in response to Mr. Hurst's invitations to submit a report on the state of the business, invariably submitted a very brief one indeed: he was, he said, raking it in.

Mr. Hurst took his mind off Julian's affairs and came back to his own.

"No," he said, in answer to Oliver's question, "I didn't see Julian last night. He was in to dinner, but he went out directly afterwards with a girl he had brought home—one I hadn't met before and I can't say I particularly wish to meet again. I don't understand why he goes out with so many different—"

"I'd better see him," said Oliver, in a tone designed to keep the discussion off family topics. "But I thought that it would come better from you."

"I didn't see him last night," went on Mr. Hurst, in the deliberate and chronological way that irritated his family so much, "but I saw him this morning.

"Oh, did you put it to him?"

"Not last night; he went out, as I said."

"What did he say?" asked Oliver.

"I saw him," said Mr. Hurst, proceeding at his own pace, "at breakfast. He came down just as I had finished mine. If I had come down to breakfast at that hour at his age, my father would have—"

"Yes, Father," Oliver slid in as gently as possible. "What did Julian think of the idea?"

"It isn't very easy to put a proposition to a man when he's standing at a sideboard throwing porridge down his throat as

6

fast as he can throw it. Besides, as I told you, I had finished my breakfast. I wanted to be on my way."

"He's a lazy devil," Oliver relaxed enough to admit. "But did you ask him, or didn't you?"

"I put it to him. I told him the facts. I said that we had an elderly client up in Yorkshire who wanted his pictures catalogued and valued, and who had written to ask us to arrange for someone to go up there. But he didn't wait for me to finish. Nobody ever does wait for the end of a sentence nowadays. He merely—"

"—went straight to the point and asked how much he'd get out of it, I suppose?"

"There!" said Mr. Hurst, in his mild, melancholy tones. "Even you do it. Conversation nowadays seems to me to be a sort of relay race: snatch and run. I find it very confusing."

Oliver found his patience running out, frowned, and then pulled himself up at the sight of the stenographer's ears which, small and neat though they were, seemed to him to be cocked at a listening angle.

"I knew you'd have difficulty," he said. "That's why I asked you to sound him out first."

"I had no difficulty," said Mr. Hurst. "You asked me to speak to him, and I did so. I didn't realize that you had put me in first, that you were using me as a battering ram."

"I thought that if you put it to him at home, casually, he'd be caught off his guard. But you can trust Julian to smell out all the snags. Did you tell him what fee Mr. Randall had offered?"

"I did."

"And he merely laughed, I suppose?"

"He remarked, with some truth, that a journey to Yorkshire in the middle of February, to catalogue some probably worthless pictures for a mere pittance—"

"Well, old Randall's a miser, as you know. You won't get him to raise it."

"No," admitted Mr. Hurst. "He's been a difficult client, on the whole, and while 'miser' is a strong word, I think he comes near enough to it to justify the use of the term. Well, we shall have to find someone else to send, that's all."

"Nonsense, Father." Oliver got off the edge of the table, stubbed out his cigarette and spoke with decision. "Nonsense. We won't get anyone—any outsider—to undertake a commission of that kind for that fee, and I can't spare anybody from the office at the moment. But I've been looking through old Randall's letter again, and I think I've found something that'll induce Julian to do the trip."

"And what is that?"

Oliver leaned over, flipped open the file on his father's desk and extracted a letter. He skimmed through it, found the line he was looking for and laid the letter before his father with one finger indicating the place.

"There," he said. "That bit about the Clauvals."

"Clauvals?" Mr. Hurst's tone was bewildered.

"I was a bit at sea myself," admitted Oliver. "I thought old Randall's handwriting had got a bit more shaky at that point, but I spent some time yesterday going into it, and I've found out what Clauvals are. I went down to old Stevens in the art shop below us, and he was full of information and enthusiasm. Clauval, he told me, was an artist who painted a very limited amount of stuff before his death—he died about twenty years ago. He doesn't seem to have got much for his pictures during his lifetime, but lately the experts have got on to them and pronounced some of them worthless and some of them near-masterpieces. I'm putting it as briefly as I can, but Stevens tells me there's something of a hunt to get hold of his better stuff. Dealers are trying to buy up all the pictures they can from unsuspecting owners who may turn out to have been harbouring some of the good Clauvals. But old Randall's too astute to be caught in that' way, and what he wants is a knowledgeable fellow who'll go and look over his collection and tell him whether he's got any of the good ones or not."

"He says"—Mr. Hurst adjusted his glasses and looked at the letter—"he says he's got some Clauvals?"

"Yes. And he's got wind of this recent rise in their value. But you can see his difficulty. Clauvals fall into two categories; some of them are worth money, some of them are not worth the canvas they're painted on. What he needs is someone who can look at his collection and tell him whether he had got any of the better stuff."

"If you'd explained that to me yesterday," said Mr. Hurst, "I would have been in a position to tell Julian—"

"If Julian's a man of business," broke in Oliver, "he'll take the chance and the pittance and the journey and see if there's anything he can pick up. Mr. Randall must have some idea of selling, and Julian would have the chance of making an offer."

Mr. Hurst glanced out at as much of the dreary weather conditions as he could see over his stenographer's back.

"I wouldn't care to motor up to Yorkshire in this weather," he commented.

"He's a bit younger than you are, sir," pointed out Oliver with some gentleness. "He'll drive up and think nothing of it—that is, if he thinks there's any good business at the other end."

9

"Well, you can sound him out," said Mr. Hurst. "He was very definite this morning, but then you hadn't told me all the facts. It might have been wiser to glean all the—"

"I had to have time to sort it out," said Oliver. "Look at that writing!"

Mr. Hurst declined to look at it, it having crossed his mind earlier that it was not unlike his own, which he thought firm and cultured.

"Very well, I'll leave it to you," he said.

"You'd better write to Randall," suggested Oliver. "Tell him we're trying to find the best man for the job. I'll go and see Julian at the shop. Do you want anything before I go?"

Mr. Hurst opened his mouth to explain that he felt that it was time for him to give up, and changed his mind as his glance fell on the stenographer's back. It wouldn't do to discuss the matter in her presence. He couldn't have it out now. He could have said anything in front of old Miss Sterndale. After twenty years there was not much that she hadn't known about the firm. She would have understood; she would have listened sympathetically; she would even have advised him—but she was gone, and things were not the same. He would wait until Oliver came in to dinner one evening, and get him alone and talk the thing over. It was better to leave it for now. He shook his head and, shuffling his papers, made his usual nervous approach to Miss Sterndale's successor.

"Er . . . Miss Er-um . . ."

Oliver closed the door behind him and, with a glance at the weather, put on his coat and scarf and drew on his warm gloves. He took a bus to Kensington and, walking up Church Street, opened the door of Aintree & Hurst, Ltd. and walked in to find the two principals absent, and the sole assistant in charge. This was a young man with little in the way of gifts, but a great deal in the way of ambition; he had saved sixty pounds towards buying a picture shop just like this one and, while waiting to add two noughts to his capital, was learning the business, polishing up his salesmanship and keeping an eye on the columns headed "Businesses for Sale." He greeted Oliver with a bow, a smile and a flourish of his duster.

"Good morning; *gooood* morning, Mr. Hurst."

It was a dreadful morning. It was bitterly cold; the sky was leaden and sleet was falling. But in the little shop with its pictures and their vivid colours, with Mervyn's glowing cheeks and red-checked duster contrasting agreeably with his dark blue suit and lemon-coloured waistcoat, it really did look a good, or at least a far better, morning.

"Nobody here, Mervyn?" enquired Oliver.

"I am here," said Mervyn, with magnificent promise. "What can I do for you, Mr. Hurst?"

"When will the others be in, do you know?"

"Mrs. Aintree came in this morning," said Mervyn. "She went out again to take a present up to Campden Hill for—"

"My God! I'd clean forgotten! It's Nannie's birthday!" exclaimed Oliver, regretting, for once, his determination to keep his father off family topics.

"'Sright," corroborated Mervyn, forgetting his dignity. "Took her up a present, Mrs. Aintree did."

"I see." Oliver stood for a few moments in thought. "Can I use the phone?"

"The phone? Certainly, *certainly*. This way, if you please," said Mervyn.

Oliver got through to his small house in Chelsea and addressed his wife with something less than his usual poise.

"Madeleine?"

"Yes? Oh, it's you, Oliver. Have you left something be-hind?"

"No; we've forgotten Nannie's birthday," he said, and heard his wife's exclamation of dismay. He had married a girl who had grown up in close friendship with the Hursts; Nannie, to Madeleine, was almost as old an institution as she was to the Hursts themselves.

"I thought I'd buy some flowers and walk up," said Oliver. "Could you go out and buy something and meet me at Camp-den Hill? Then it would look as though—"

"All right," said Madeleine. "But if I'm going out, I think I'll stay out. Will you take me to lunch somewhere?"

"Well, I could, yes," said Oliver, with the deliberation of a man who has been married for six years. "If we didn't hang it out too long."

"Don't be too enthusiastic," said Madeleine. " 'Bye; see you at Campden Hill."

Oliver left the shop, bought a large and expensive bunch of flowers and walked up to the house in which he and his brother and sister had been born and which he had left only upon his marriage.

The big, square house on Campden Hill had been built by an Alfred Hurst in the first half of the nineteenth cen-tury. It had a name, Greenmount, and even an address, four-teen Hillmount Gardens, but the Hursts referred to it simply by the name of the district in which it stood, Campden Hill. It was well and solidly built and had been well and solidly furnished; the cupboards were vast, the chairs and sofas gar-gantuan and the bedroom furniture almost immovable. Each succeeding Hurst bride had come to the house with plans for redecorating and refurnishing, and each had been com-pelled by sheer weight to abandon the schemes. They had concentrated, instead, on installing the latest warming or labour-saving devices, with the result that the house had a warmth and comfort seldom met in dwellings of the size and period.

It had been, for generations, the custom for the eldest son to set up a home of his own upon his marriage and return to Campden Hill on the death of his father; a suite of rooms on the ground floor was reserved for the dowager, and here the widow, if there was a widow, would retire to spend the remainder of her days. The suite had, at present, no occupant; Edwin's wife would have liked to move into it, since it would not only have saved her the journeys up and down stairs to her bedroom, but would also have been nearer to the kitchen, in which a large part of her time was passed. She had not yet made the suggestion, however; she was still trying to think of suitable words in which to ask her husband whether he would object to her moving into the widow's quarters.

Oliver walked up to the house with the pleasant feeling of home-coming with which he always approached it; he still thought of it, and referred to it, as home. He liked his own little house in Chelsea, but he would not have dreamed of keeping it on after his father's death. He pushed open the big iron gate and, walking up the drive, went round to the side of the house and let himself in by the library door. He then went to the kitchen, where he was almost certain of finding his mother.

She was not in the kitchen, but she was not far away; she was sitting with her sister, Mrs. Aintree, at a table in the adjoining room which, once a butler's pantry, had lately been converted into a dining room in convenient proximity to the kitchen.

"Hello, Mother." Oliver bent and kissed her. "Hello, Aunt Rowena."

"Good morning, Oliver," said Mrs. Hurst. "Coffee?"

"Thanks. Hadn't I better go in and see Nannie first?"

"No. Julian's with her; she'll enjoy you better one at a time."

"Nice flowers," said his aunt, studying them. "And by my troth, costly. That means that you forgot the day."

Her voice, in contrast to his mother's slow and even tones, was incisive and had sardonic undertones. The two women, though somewhat alike in appearance, were far from similar in character. Both were good-looking, but Mrs. Hurst was a quiet, domesticated woman of just over fifty, whose interest in her own appearance began and ended with a desire to look neat. She was a level-headed and a patient woman, keeping together, with good sense and good humour, a family of widely varying and sometimes difficult temperaments. Her interests centred round her home and family; she disliked bridge, detested parties and had reduced her circle of friends to a chosen few who made no demands upon her time. She liked housework, enjoyed cooking and never opened a newspaper until she needed it to wrap up the garbage. She lived a life which, by some standards, was one of quiet usefulness, by others, one of complete stagnation.

Mrs. Aintree was forty-four, handsome and always beautifully dressed in black relieved by gleams and flashes. She had, after a short and unsuccessful marriage, occupied herself in a variety of business projects, the latest of which was the opening of the Church Street shop in partnership with her nephew, Julian. She lived in a flat at Hampstead, and had a great many men friends, with whom she remained on good terms until they became what she termed familiar, when she instantly dismissed them. As her good looks and good humour attracted men, and as her free-and-easy manner roused in them expectations of the most delicious kind, it came about that Julian had to deal with a great many bewildered gentlemen who, finding Mrs. Aintree's door barred to them, sought her in the shop and tried to find out how and when they had erred.

"How," Oliver asked her as he sat down to his coffee, "does the shop manage to be so prosperous when you and Julian spend so much of your time away from it?"

"Not shop," said Mrs. Aintree. "Studio, salon, gallery—but not shop, if you please."

"Well, whatever it is, it runs itself."

"Organization," said Mrs. Aintree. "A thing I'm always trying to teach your mother. If she organized, she wouldn't have to spend all her time in the kitchen."

"Well, no; I could cook in one of the other rooms," said Mrs. Hurst. "Oliver, is Madeleine coming?"

"Yes. How's Drusilla?"

Drusilla was much in everybody's mind at the moment. She was the youngest of the three Hursts; Oliver was thirty, Julian twenty-seven and Drusilla twenty-three. She had been married for just over a year to a young man who was at once a peer and an officer in the famous regiment of Guards; he had been sent abroad and Drusilla was on the point of going with him when she found that she was to have a baby. Lord Cuffy, therefore, went out without his wife, and Drusilla was hoping to join him with their son or daughter. She had gone about her preparations for the baby with such vigour that now, with two months still to wait, she had nothing to do; all was ready—except the baby, and Drusilla was experiencing what she would have called, in other circumstances, a

15

feeling of flatness. She was living at home, though a great part of her time was spent at the house in Chelsea discussing technical details with her sister-in-law, Madeleine, who, having a son of four and a half, was felt by Drusilla to be qualified to give more up-to-date information than Mrs. Hurst could.

"Drusilla's very well," answered her mother. "At least, she's well in health, but she gets a bit low in spirits. It's hard for her, not having Cuffy here just when she needs him most."

"Has she decided to have it at home?" asked Oliver.

"No, I've fixed things up at the nursing home."

"Quite right, too," said Mrs. Aintree, who had never had any children and had never been in a nursing home. "Much more sensible than filling the house with a lot of starchy nurses all running everybody off their feet. They— Oh, here's Nannie!"

"Well, Nannie." Oliver, rising, went over and kissed her. "Many happy returns of the day."

Nannie was a tall, angular woman with a rich voice and an accent which was the heritage of a Lancashire father and a Somerset mother. She had come to Mrs. Hurst as a girl of eighteen to look after Oliver, then one year old, while his own highly trained but unsatisfactory nurse was on holiday. The nurse had never returned, an omission which Mrs. Hurst had found increasing reason to bless as the years went by. She had entrusted the care of all three children to Nannie, and Nannie had brought them up upon lines which had done very well for her own upbringing and which she felt would do very well for the little Hursts. It was a method sound but unorthodox. While their friends were being psychoanalyzed and encouraged to express themselves freely, the three juvenile Hursts were enjoined to save their breath to cool their broth, to eat up their crusts to make their hair curl, to keep their ears open and their mouths shut, and to come when they were called and shut the door after them. Kensington Gardens, accustomed to gentle admonitions, "I wouldn't do that if I were you, darling," shook, and the Round Pond rippled under "Stop that naow, you great ninny you, if you don't want a roight good smack on the seat." The children came to school age and passed out of her care, and Nannie now shared with Mrs. Hurst the work of the house. She remained Nannie to everybody, and her methods continued simple and direct. Cuffy himself—the first peer who had ever shown any disposition to ally himself with a daughter of the Hursts—was told, without ceremony, to "wipe your boots on the front-door mat and not on the drawing-room carpet, you great silly you." Her simplicity in a world which was digging feverishly below the surface to find Freudian explanations for every desire or preference, kept the family sane in outlook and young in heart.

On this, her forty-eighth birthday, Nannie had scant time for speeches.

"All that money on a great bew-kay of flowers, that you'd have got out of the garden for nothing!" she told Oliver. "And patience cards!" she exclaimed, on unwrapping Rowena's present. "Glory be! Patience cards! How old do you think Oi am? Oi'm forty-eight, not nointy-eight! And when'll Oi foind the toime to sit and play cards, with all the work piling up all round and nothing getting done! Patience cards! Well, Oi don't doubt it was well meant."

"I bought them for you because I was going to *teach* you how to play," explained Rowena, somewhat dashed. "We were talking about you the other day, and we all thought it would be a good thing if you were off your feet sometimes, playing—"

"Patience! Whatever next?" asked Nannie in wonderment. "Oi used to see old Granny Hurst at it—Oi thought, you old slowpoke you, sitting down there playing with all them silly little pictures when you could be doing something useful, loike knitting coats for Mrs. Oliver's baby what was on the way then. Well, Oi moight come to it in toime. In thirty years toime, perhaps."

Madeleine, arriving a few moments later and joining the party in the kitchen, kissed her mother-in-law and then presented her gift to Nannie; since there had been no time for consultation, nobody but Nannie was surprised to find two packs of patience cards reposing in the box.

"Why, you've given me the same's Mrs. Aintree's just given me, you great silly you!" exclaimed Nannie. "Why didn't you buy me a noice, warm pair of gloves, naow? If you'd asked me, Oi would have told you Oi wanted them, secret-loike."

"You shall have your gloves, Nannie darling," declared Madeleine. "What did Julian and Drusilla give you?"

"Drusilla, she hasn't come downstairs yet, the great lazy," said Nannie. "Julian, he's going to take me out to give me a treat, he says, to one of them places where they wait on you and give you food you could get better and cheaper and cleaner at home. Here they are naow."

Julian came in with his sister, and at the sight of them something deep stirred in both Mrs. Hurst and Nannie. Though Nannie would have turned roundly upon anybody who said that she had a favourite, it was certain that Drusilla had a place in her affections larger than either of the boys. Mrs. Hurst, more introspective, knew that Julian was her

18

darling, and knew that Julian knew it. She loved all her children, and she had treated them with scrupulous fairness, but in Oliver she saw a touch of his father's dullness without his father's compensating sweetness; Drusilla was amusing but self-absorbed. Only in Julian did she find the perfect degree of companionship. She told herself that he was spoilt and arrogant, but she knew that he had more humour, charm and intelligence than Oliver and Drusilla put together. Julian was her pride; looking at him, she could never decide whether the pride lay in him for being what he was, or in herself for being his mother.

"Dru's got a present for you, Nannie," he said, ushering his sister into the room. "Come on, Dru, fork it out."

Drusilla, her soft, fair hair in disarray, was in a housecoat which, loose and flowing though it was, could not disguise the lines of her figure. She put her arms round Nannie's neck and hugged her.

"Here you are, Nannie," she said, handing over her present. "Many happy returns."

"Patience cards, Oi'll be bound," said Nannie.

"Yes, how did you— Oh!" wailed Drusilla in dismay, "did somebody else give you some, too?"

"Next year, it'll be a crop of bath chairs, Oi reckon," said Nannie. "Never mind, dearie, Oi dare say Oi'll be able to use 'em all some day, if Oi live long enough. My goodness, we're a crowd in here! Go on naow, all of you, and let's get some peace to get on with the work."

She gathered the coffee cups on to a tray and carried them to the kitchen, and there was a general movement among the others to put birthdays aside and pursue the business of the day.

"Don't go for a minute," Oliver asked his brother. "I'd like a word with you."

"No ball," said Julian, instantly. "No. Father tried it this morning and I told him there was nothing doing. You can't take me away from my own business and send me off to do a silly job that one of your clerks could do on his head. I can't leave the shop, anyhow. Aunt Rowena's only the sleeping partner. I'm the prop, the mainstay; I'm the brains. I'm the—"

"Trumpeter, what are you sounding now?" his aunt wanted to know. "And who wants you to go where?"

"Oliver's talking about that trip again," said Julian. "I told you, the old man who wants his pictures sorted out."

"No, he can't go, Oliver," pronounced Rowena. "Send up one of your own staff and leave mine alone. Good gracious, anyone can sort out a few pictures and list them; why send someone like Julian up there to do it?"

"Because I thought he'd be interested, that's all," said Oliver.

"Interested in what?" asked Julian. "A lot of pictures that were taken by this Randall fellow to a new house and stacked in one room and left there for the past God knows how many years. He didn't even bother to hang them. Father told me himself that there was nothing of the smallest value. Junk. I know exactly what there'll be: sepia reproductions of *Bubbles* and *The Laughing Cavalier* and *Dignity* and *Impudence*. I could make out the list without ever going near the place."

"There are some Clauvals," said Oliver.

"Some—? How do you know?" demanded his aunt.

"Mr. Randall says so in his letter."

"What are Clauvals?" enquired Madeleine, interrupting her conversation with Drusilla.

"Clauval," explained Oliver, in his slow, somewhat heavy way, "is an artist. Was an artist. He's been dead some years, but he interests people like Julian because some of his work is rubbish and some of it, the experts have discovered recently, is very good. There aren't many, it's thought, of the good ones, and dealers have been buying them lately and making a pretty good profit on them."

"Where did he get all that knowledge?" asked Rowena in wonder.

"Out of old Stevens, I bet," said Julian.

"Quite right," said Oliver. "I went down and talked to him. He says that if you don't go, he'll send a man up himself."

There was a pause, during which two of the listeners wondered whether there was any truth in this statement.

"He's lying," said Julian, at last.

"Probably, but it's a risk, isn't it?" his aunt asked him.

"You can go to old Stevens yourself," offered Oliver. "I really can't see why Julian's making so much fuss at a trip that needn't take him more than a week, and that might bring you both some business. I can't spare a man at the moment and even if I could, he wouldn't know whether the Clauvals that Mr. Randall mentions are the good ones or the bad ones. I've got to send somebody; the fee's low, but Randall is one of our oldest clients and we wouldn't like to lose him."

"Where does he live?" asked Mrs. Hurst.

"It's 'way up in the frozen north," said Julian. "A place called—called what, Oliver? Oh, Holside. I've looked it up; more accurately, Father looked it up for me this morning.

It's in Yorkshire, one of those villages tucked away in the dales—I think they call them dales, don't they? This place is halfway up a hill, anyway, with a nice view of open moorland, which might be all right in midsummer but which doesn't tempt me at this time of the year."

"You could toboggan," said Madeleine.

"Thank you," said Julian. "I think I can do without—"

"It would be annoying," broke in Rowena thoughtfully, "if there *were* some good Clauvals up there, and we missed them. Two people have come into the shop lately and asked for Clauvals and I've had to say we hadn't got a single work to show them. Perhaps you'd better go, Julian."

"In the summer," promised Julian.

"But good Heavens," protested his aunt, "you think nothing of driving all the way up to your godmother's in the middle of winter, and she's twice, three times, as far as this Holside place."

"That's different," said Julian. "There's some point in going up to Blairwhinnie. Nobody minds driving up to a house that's two miles from a skiing club, and in the loveliest part of Scotland. There'd be something to go *for*. I'd—"

"Then why not *go*?" exclaimed Rowena. "Why not write to your godmother and ask her to arrange one of those nice parties for you, with outdoor girls to ski with and indoor girls to dance with? You could tell her that you're a third of the way to Blairwhinnie, and she'd have one of her nice house parties like last year. You know how much you always enjoy going there; you told me it was as good as Switzerland and a good deal cheaper. You needn't take long over this Mr. Randall; you can go on to Blairwhinnie and have a wonderful time and—" She broke off and stared at Drusilla, who was showing unmistakable signs of dissolving into tears. "What's the matter, Dru?" she asked. "Have I said something?"

"She and Cuffy were there last year," explained Mrs. Hurst. "Don't worry, Drusilla, there'll be lots of other nice times."

"We had such *fun*," said Drusilla, wiping her eyes. "And now I'm stuck here, looking terrible, and C-Cuffy's thousands and th-thousands of miles away. Don't you remember, Julian? We had the most wonderful—"

"It was pretty good," said Julian. "It mightn't be a bad idea to write and say I'm going up."

Oliver's expression changed subtly; he took his coat from the back of a chair and shrugged himself into it. The look on his brother's face told him that he would go to Scotland; it was reasonable to assume that he would take in Mr. Randall on the way.

"Well, Mother, I'll be going," he said.

"Hang on; I'll come with you," said Julian.

"Before you go, Julian, will you do the boiler, please?" asked his mother.

"The boiler?" echoed Julian, aghast. "Oh, Mother, not now! Why can't the gardener do it?"

"Because he's new and he doesn't understand it. He's waiting for you to show him what he's doing wrong. Do go on, Julian, please. The house isn't nearly as warm as it should be. You don't want your father to have to do it, do you?"

"Yes," said Julian. "Well, not Father, particularly, just anyone. Why can't Oliver come and live at home again? I get all the boiler missions nowadays."

Mrs. Aintree rose to her feet and picked up her gloves and handbag.

"Well, business is business," she said, "and we can do with a Clauval or two. Julian, you'll have to go to Holside."

"All right, I'll go," said Julian, "but I'll lay a heavy bet before I go that as far as Clauvals are concerned, it'll be a wild goose chase."

"If you'll come to the office with me," said Oliver, "I'll give you all the details."

"No, not the office," said Julian. "I'm like Father, I prefer the old place, even if the stairs did give me palpitations. Once I got up there, I could see you or Father in reasonable privacy, with only poor old doddery Susie Sterndale looking on. I went to the main door of the new place once, and found myself staring through a glass door at wide open spaces. What made you go in for that kind of décor?"

"A desire for light and air and cheerfulness," said Oliver. "Besides, I can see what the staff's doing now."

"What did you do with poor old Susie?"

"Miss Sterndale was honourably retired on an adequate pension," said Oliver.

"Poor old Miss Sterndale," said Mrs. Hurst. "Your father's lost without her."

"Nonsense, Mother," said Oliver. "He's got a perfectly good stenographer and he'll soon get used to her."

"Well, I hope so," said Mrs. Hurst. "Will you all go away, please? I've got work to do."

"What's for lunch, Mother?" asked Julian.

"Rissoles," she said.

"Not if I know it," said Julian. "I shall go and—"

"Oh, Julian," broke in Drusilla, "I tell you what, Madeleine and I are going shopping—we're going to change the patience cards—and then we're meeting Oliver. Can't we all have lunch together at your club?"

"At my—" There was a notable lack of enthusiasm in Julian's tone. "Not at my club."

"Why not?" demanded Drusilla. "We often have."

"Yes, but not—er—lately," said Julian. "I mean, why not wait until—"

"He's trying to get out of it," said Drusilla. "He's—Oh! He's ashamed of the way I look!"

"No, for Pete's sake, Drusilla," began Julian, "I—"

"Then *why* can't we go to your club?"

"Well," said Julian, driven into a corner, "I only thought for your sake, that you'd be less embarrassed if—"

"What do you expect me to do?" asked Drusilla, on a rising note. "Creep out at night, like cats?"

"Certainly not. I merely—"

"You *are* ashamed! You are! Just because I look—"

"Oh, Julian, you are a pig!" said Madeleine. "You've gone and upset her."

"I do wish you'd learn tact," said Mrs. Hurst.

"I didn't say a thing!" protested Julian. "I never do say a thing! I don't know why she cries every time I open my mouth."

"You're a blundering idiot," his aunt informed him. "You've hurt her feelings."

"Hurt her—! I didn't say a word about staying in until it was dark! She's got to go out, everybody knows that! I'm not blaming her; I know she can't help looking the size of a house and—"

"Oh!" wailed the stricken Drusilla. "You b-beast! It's bad enough to know it without being told it!"

"Don't mind him; he's a heavy-footed, brainless, worthless and witless moron," said Rowena. "Go on upstairs and change into some nice warm things, Dru, and then you and

Madeleine can go out and do a nice morning's shopping and you'll feel better."

"Come on," said Oliver to his brother. "You've worn your welcome out."

The two went out together, and Julian stood in the hall putting on his coat.

"Damn fuss over nothing," he muttered.

"You ought to tread a bit more delicately just at the moment," advised Oliver. "It's a boring time for Drusilla. How would you like to look like that?"

"Well, there's not much likelihood," said Julian.

"What about coming to the office, after all, and looking over that letter of Randall's?"

"No, not the office," said Julian. "You can give me the details later. I'll meet you for lunch."

"At your club?"

"I suppose so. If I say 'no' and the baby's born with a squint, everybody'll say it was my fault. Look, will you get the two girls to a table? I'll come in and join you a bit later. You're a family man, you won't mind sailing down the dining room looking as though you were responsible."

"All right," agreed Oliver. "It'll be interesting," he added, "to see you with a wife of your own."

"When I'm thirty," said Julian. "Not a day before. See you about one-fifteen." He walked back a few steps and yelled towards the kitchen. *"Mo-ther!"*

"What is it?" came faintly, from afar.

"Shan't be home for *lunch*," yelled Julian. "Having it with the *gardener* in the *boiler*."

Chapter 2

A WEEK LATER Julian was getting ready for his journey north. As Oliver had foreseen, he was going on a visit to his godmother and taking in Mr. Randall on the way. His appeals for assistance with his packing had been ignored, but when Nannie had climbed the stairs three times in order to prove that his shirts, vests and pajamas were where she had said they were; when Mrs. Hurst had gone up and down stairs several times on missions connected with cleaning and pressing; when Drusilla, letting bygones be bygones, had gone up to one of the attics and brought down her husband's skiing outfit with a view to lending it to her brother, it was felt that the wise course would be to do Julian's task for him and get him out of the house as quickly as possible. His suitcases were therefore filled neatly, a flask of hot coffee provided for his refreshment on the road and a packet of sandwiches placed ready to his hand in the car. His luggage and equipment were stowed under his supervision, and the traveller was then ready to depart.

"Mother, did you pack my polo sweater?" he asked anxiously.

"I packed everything," said Mrs. Hurst. "I do wish you'd go, Julian. We've wasted half the morning getting you ready."

"Go along, you great helpless you," said Nannie, banging the car door on the last package and bustling indoors. "Go along, do. Drusilla, you come inside out of the cold."

"Coming," said Drusilla. "Julian, look after Cuffy's things, won't you?"

"Yes, yes, yes," said Julian, absently. "Where did I put that map?"

"It's here," said his mother. "Drive carefully, won't you? The roads are sure to be treacherous in this weather."

"Yes, yes, yes," murmured Julian, his finger following a route on the opened map. "Here we are: Great North Road as far as Doncaster, I think and then a straight line up through York. Or I might keep on A-1 and go off it just here. It all depends."

"It'll be nice country once you get into the hills," said Drusilla.

"It'll be nice if you can see it," said Julian, "but those Yorkshire mists are a lot thicker than the Scottish ones—and a lot wetter, too. 'Bye, Mother. 'Bye, Dru, let me know if the baby jumps the gun, and I'll send down a nice parcel of Yorkshire parkin for him—or her, or both."

He started the engine, waved a hand and was off, and the two women stared after him thoughtfully.

"Selfish pigs, men," said Drusilla. "I suppose if Cuffy didn't have someone to look after his things, I'd have to do

28

what we've done this morning—brush and press and sort and pack, while he just sat there. I do think women are wonderful, Mother, don't you?"

"Yes, I do," said Mrs. Hurst.

"But we ought to have told Julian to go to the devil and do his own packing, oughtn't we?"

"I suppose so."

"But if we had, he would have done it in the end quite efficiently, and then gone off and left his room looking like the wrath of God, for us to clean up."

"That is so."

"And for the first few days, we'd leave it, and then it would get on our nerves and we'd go in and get it nice and tidy for him again, wouldn't we?"

"I'm afraid we would," said Mrs. Hurst. "Let's go indoors before we both get pneumonia."

Julian, glancing at his clock when he was out of the heavy town traffic, saw that it was almost noon. An hour later, he was making steady progress up the Great North Road and settling down to several hours of driving. The weather was at first reasonably good, but near Stamford it began to deteriorate, and by the time he reached Newark snow was falling heavily and a thickening mist was reducing his speed. Nearing Doncaster he decided not to leave the main highway; the mist was bad here, but it would be worse in the low areas round York.

By the time he reached Boroughbridge road conditions were so bad that he pulled into a roadside garage and had chains affixed to his wheels; after this, he found he made better speed, but a little later the mist came down heavily and slowed him down, at moments, to walking pace.

His state of mind, cheerful enough at the start of the journey, began, like the weather, to worsen considerably. He felt more and more strongly that he had been, as usual, too impulsive; he had thought too much about the house party in Scotland and not nearly enough about the intervening days in Yorkshire which, he felt now, were not going to be at all to his liking.

Julian Hurst was a young man who took very much for granted the good things which life had brought him. He was not given to introspection; if he had mused at all upon his circumstances, he would have decided that he was luckier than most, and left it at that. He was a member of a class which, though wealthy, had no great burden of possession to drain their resources; they owned the houses they lived in, the cars they drove; they lived well but moderately. What they wanted, they could, as a rule, easily afford, but they were comfort- rather than pleasure-loving.

Julian had come to take comfort as a matter of course. He lived in a comfortable and well-warmed house; he was well fed, well looked after, but apart from donations which he sent off secretly and somewhat shamefacedly during the Christmas season, he showed no awareness that his lot, compared with that of the majority of his fellow-men, was cast in very pleasant places indeed. His code, if he could be said to have one, included paying his bills promptly, going to Holy Communion on the two days of the year on which he could be certain that all his friends would go too, and behaving towards women exactly as each wished him to behave. If he had an idea that he was not, on the whole, any worse than the next fellow, it did not amount to a conviction; it was vague and fleeting and at all times unacknowledged.

He found, on his journey, that the farther north he went, the more he wished that he were going south. He did not care for the north of England at any time, and he had never imagined that he would be going, in midwinter, to a part of the country that even in summer he would have avoided. Though he was on a main road, he saw few signs of other vehicles; he felt alone in a waste of snow; everybody else, he decided, was wisely keeping off the road and only fools like himself were abroad.

He had long ago abandoned his hopeful intention of arriving at Mr. Randall's house in the pleasant hour between tea and dinner; darkness was falling and he was getting into country which he knew little and, under these circumstances, liked less. He saw the lights of a village through the mist and, driving the car into the courtyard of an inn that looked like a design for a Christmas card, went inside, sought the proprietor and asked him some questions about the district for which he was bound.

The answers were not encouraging; the road to Holside seemed to be the one which, under winter conditions, was the first to disappear and the last to reappear.

"You'd do better to stay the night and go on in the morning," suggested the proprietor.

Julian hesitated. It would perhaps be more sensible, but on the other hand, whatever the weather threatened, the clock showed that it was still early enough to go on and reach Holside in time for dinner. Pleasant as the inn looked, Julian had in his mind a far more attractive picture: the great hall of a mellow country mansion, with a log fire blazing and a good dinner in prospect. He had taken the precaution of telegraphing a day ahead; he was expected, and his room would be ready for him. Whatever difficulties he encountered on the way—and, once he got on to the Holside

31

road, they might be considerable—he would find himself well repaid at the journey's end.

"I'll go on, I think—thanks," he said.

It was slow going for the next few miles, but the roads appeared to have been cleared of snow earlier in the day, and the surface was good. He was beginning to feel the strain of driving through the thick mist; the roads were no longer straight, but wound round the foot of the hills. Sometimes Julian found himself climbing steeply; at others, he was going as steeply down.

Holside, when he eventually reached it, proved to be a village built partly on the level of the road and partly on the shoulder of a hill; it was upon this shoulder that Mr. Randall's house stood, and Julian, after getting out to ask the way, drove through the lower village and followed the road up the hill—and from that moment, found himself with no time to think of anything but driving; all his energies were concentrated in keeping himself in the driver's seat and the car on the winding track. Somewhere at the back of his mind was a grateful acknowledgement of the car's performance. She was, he realized, doing her wonderful best; she seemed to be feeling her way along with an uncanny knowledge of the worse pitfalls of the dreadful surface.

Mr. Randall's house, Holside Manor, was the last of four houses built beyond the upper village; Julian peered out and saw the lights of the first house and crept along: one house, two, and then the third. There appeared to be no fourth house; Julian, backing cautiously, started once more at the first one, but after the third, lowered the window and, seeing a muffled figure in the gloom, shouted a question.

"Am I right for Holside Manor?"

"Yes," came the reply. "Straight on, next house."

"Thanks." Julian drove on, but he looked in vain for any gleam in the darkness. The first sign of the house was not a row of brightly lit windows, not an illuminated porch or even a chink of light from a cheerful room, it was a pair of tall, wrought-iron gates which he glimpsed just as he had driven past them. Julian stopped, reversed and cursed bitterly as he saw that there was no sign of a lodge from which anyone might spring—even on such a night—to open them. He got out, put his shoulder to them, pushed them back with an energy born of anger and then got into the car and drove along a short gravel approach, bringing the car to a stop before a large house in which there was not the slightest sign of light or even of life.

Too surprised to do more than stare out at it through the murky darkness, Julian sat motionless for some minutes. Then a sound came to his ears, and he switched off the engine and listened until it came again. He had been right; somewhere at the side of the house, a door had opened and closed again. The place was at least occupied.

On reaching this conclusion, Julian opened the car door and got out with an air of purpose. It was too dark for anybody to see his expression, even if anybody had been there to look, but Oliver would have seen signs that his normally even-tempered brother was very angry.

Before lifting out the single suitcase which he would need here, Julian paused to do some thinking. This was without doubt the right house, and Mr. Randall must have had his telegram. He was later than he expected to be, but it was still not yet eight o'clock—a reasonable enough hour in view of the difficult driving conditions. In spite of this, the gates had been closed and no attempt had been made to guide him by even one light.

33

Running over his brother's description of Mr. Randall, Julian saw for the first time that it had a vagueness, a sketchiness which, he now realized, was deliberate. He assembled certain scattered items which, put together, made a picture with a notable lack of attractive features. Oliver had, he realized now, issued his information piecemeal: a word here, a hint there, thrown out with a lifelong knowledge of his brother's habitual disdain for details in any matter that did not greatly interest him. It was not the first time he had used the knowledge; Julian, standing in the snow, recognized and saluted his brother's duplicity and chalked up another score to be settled between them. He had, he told himself grimly, been had for a mug; as for brotherly treatment, this was only another of those coat-of-many-colours affairs; here he was, in Egypt, and he had no one to blame but himself.

He had still to find out whether Mr. Randall knew he was coming, or didn't know he was coming, or didn't care. It was unlikely that he was away from home; he had written to London and asked for a man to be sent up, and the man was here.

Putting an end to speculation, Julian stepped up to the front door and looked round for a bell or a knocker. Feeling his way down the wall, his hand brushed against a rope, and he seized it and gave it a sharp tug. The next moment he leapt several feet off the ground at the shattering peal that sounded almost in his ear. He was still recovering from its effects when the door opened and the reason for the force of the summons became at once evident: the manservant standing before him was very old, and very deaf. With a motion indicating his lack of hearing, he admitted Julian and gave him a brief, old-fashioned bow.

"Good evening, sir. Mr. Hurst?"

34

"Yes."

"Mr. Randall is expecting you."

A lift of one eyebrow was Julian's only comment on this statement. Without speaking, he allowed the man to help him off with his coat, and followed him through the large dimly-lit hall, down a wide corridor and to the door of a room on the left. Opening the door, the servant stepped inside and announced the visitor.

"Mr. Julian Hurst, sir."

"Ah."

There was no welcome in the monosyllable. It was uttered from the depths of a high-backed chair close to one of the most miserable fires Julian had ever looked upon; nothing was visible of the speaker save a pair of claw-like hands that gripped the arms of the chair. The servant withdrew, and Julian advanced until he reached a point at which he could both see and be seen by his host; then he stopped and, seeing that he himself was being subjected to a silent head-to-foot survey, allowed himself the privilege of studying in his turn the extraordinary figure seated in the chair.

Mr. Randall was eighty-two, and though the lines upon his face were not deep for a man of his years, the head upon which Julian was looking was completely bald, a rounded, gleaming dome. In sharp contrast to his exposed scalp, the rest of Mr. Randall was hidden from view by a thick suit, woollen underwear which protruded at his wrists and ankles, a Shetland shawl which was thrown over his shoulders and a thick rug which lay across his knees. Thus muffled, he had the appearance of a rare species of bear, and this, together with the bare dome, solved for ever in Julian's mind the question raised by the rhyme as to whether Fuzzy Wuzzy was or wasn't fuzzy.

35

Mr. Randall made no attempt to share the fire; having ended his appraisal of his visitor, he addressed him.

"So there y'are, young fellow," he said.

"How do you do?" said Julian, adding, after some calculation, a cool "sir."

"Sit down," ordered Mr. Randall, indicating a chair.

Julian, with a glance at the depressing-looking fire, drew a chair, with some ostentation, as close to the warmth as he could, and Mr. Randall gave an impatient cluck.

"If it's a great roaring blaze you're looking for, all going up into the chimney, young man," he said, in a high soft tone, "you won't find it here." He peered round at Julian. "D'you know—have you any idea at all what it costs to heat a house of this size?"

"It must be expensive," admitted Julian.

"That's why I don't do it," said Mr. Randall. His voice, though high, was perfectly steady. "I won't do it. There are nine rooms on this floor alone; above this, you've got five bedrooms and above that again, more rooms and lofts and attics. If you think I'm going to keep a furnace going to warm an entire house when I only occupy two rooms in it, you're very much mistaken. You'll find a fire in your bedroom and a fire in the North Room—that's where the pictures are, and that's where you'll spend most of your time. I'll tell you what I've brought you here to do, and then you can do it in your own time. I shan't see you until you've done it. I'm an old man, but I'm a busy man; I've got the finest collection of coins—with the exception of two—in the country, and I'm still adding to it. That takes all m'time and all m'strength. Now, don't say anything, but just listen while I tell you what you're here for. You wouldn't be here at all if your father hadn't given me his guarantee that you're qualified to do the job. Now. I've got some pictures. A lot of pictures, most of them valueless. I brought them to this house when I came to it over twenty years ago, and I had them stacked in the North Room; I never troubled to have them put up. Now I want them looked over and listed. Among them, you'll find some by this fellow who's been taken up recently by the art know-alls. If you think they're worth anything, I'll sell them. The rest can stay in the North Room until I die and they bury me; I'm not going to the trouble and expense of sending them to sales. You can start work tomorrow. Nobody'll disturb you; there's nobody in the house except m'self and the butler and a cook of sorts. You won't see me until you come and report that the job's done. I live on this floor and so does the butler; I never go upstairs, can't manage 'em now. The butler's old, but he's not doddering; he'll look after you. You'll have your breakfast in your bedroom and your other meals in the North Room. When you've got through the work, you can come and see me and I'll give you your cheque. Have I made everything clear?"

"Perfectly clear," said Julian.

"Then I shall say good night to you. Will you kindly take my stick and bang it on the floor of the passage outside? Biscoe—that's the butler—doesn't hear bells. If you want him, you must knock on the floor of your room and he'll generally hear you."

Julian rose and, without a word, took Mr. Randall's stick and, walking out of the room, banged vigorously on the floor outside. Returning, he gave the stick back to its owner and then stood waiting until the sound of footsteps told him that Biscoe was approaching.

"Biscoe," said Mr. Randall, when the man appeared, "take Mr. Hurst up to his room."

37

The gesture accompanying the words was sufficient to make the speaker's meaning clear; Biscoe led the visitor to the door. Julian, before going out, turned and spoke in an expressionless voice to his host.

"Good night, Mr. Randall."

"Good night to you."

The door closed. Julian found himself following the butler towards the stairs; as they reached them, he paused and glanced towards the front door, and the meaning of the glance was plain: he could walk out now, he could go away and go north or south, to his godmother's home or to his own. He could go back to comfort and the society of people who understood the alphabet of politeness. He could—

"I have taken your suitcase upstairs, sir," said a gentle voice behind him.

Julian turned and looked at the old butler, at the thin, stooping form, the handsome white head and the mild, wise old eyes. After a few moments, he smiled.

"Thank you," he said. "If you'll tell me where the garage is, I'll put the car away."

He returned to the house to find the old man waiting for him. He followed him up the stairs and along a wide corridor on the first floor. Biscoe opened the door of a room and Julian, entering, found that it was large, sparsely furnished and bitterly cold.

"Mr. Randall doesn't care to have the fires lit too early, sir," said Biscoe. "This one will soon burn up nicely, and I've left you a full scuttle of coal. Mr. Randall thought you would like your dinner in here tonight, sir. What time would you care to have it?"

"Oh, at once, I think," said Julian.

He spoke in an ordinary tone, and saw with relief that

38

the man followed, with apparent ease, the movement of his lips. He felt somewhat relieved; at least he would not have to shout whenever he had to ask for anything.

"The bathroom, sir," went on Biscoe, "is the second door on the left. The water is hottest at about nine o'clock in the evening, sir, so if I may suggest—"

"All right; I'll have a bath last thing every night," said Julian.

"Very good, sir. Is there anything you require now?"

Julian looked round. His suitcase had vanished; his clothes had been put away, his pajamas were laid neatly on the bed and the bed-clothes were turned back in readiness for the night.

"Nothing more, thanks."

The old man went out of the room and the door closed quietly behind him. Julian, walking to the fireplace, picked up the coal scuttle and flung half its contents on to the fire. This done, he stood watching it moodily, reviewing the events of the day. The drive had been tiring, but a warm welcome or at least a warm fire and the offer of a drink would have dispelled fatigue and brought in its place a pleasing languor and sense of well-being. There had not, however, been even the pretence of a welcome; he had been admitted, marched into the presence, harangued and sent up to his room to have his bath and go to bed. The prospect before him was, he considered, one of unalleviated blackness. He was to stay in the North Room, alone, freezing and practically unattended. Certainly being alone was, he considered, preferable to seeing any more of his hairless host, but the outlook, on the whole, was grim, and it behooved him to skim with the utmost speed through the work of sorting and listing the pictures, submit his report and depart as soon as he could.

He undressed rapidly and, putting on a dressing gown, went into the corridor and walked towards the second door on the left. He opened the bathroom door, entered, shivered and was about to shut it after him when he noticed with astonishment that the room opposite appeared to be occupied. The bed was ready for an occupant and the fire—a low and miserable fire, with little cheerfulness about it—was burning in the grate. Julian shut the bathroom door and, turning on the hot water tap and finding with relief that it bore out its name, sat on the edge of the bath tub and speculated upon the occupant of the room opposite. Mr. Randall had told him that he and the butler lived on the ground floor; he had also said that they were alone. There was a cook, but it was not likely that a cook would be permitted by Mr. Randall to live in one of the best bedrooms and enjoy the luxury of a fire.

Musing over the little mystery as he bathed, Julian forgot it in the course of a brisk towelling and a sharpening desire for food. That was his bath over, he reflected; now he would go and eat his dinner, see what could be done about a drink and then settle down to an early night.

Back in his room, he was agreeably surprised to find that a table had been drawn up close to the fire, and a clean cloth, silver and china laid upon it. Two or three dishes were keeping warm on a stand near the blaze; exploring without too much hope, Julian found, to his delight, a steaming rabbit pie, potatoes and Brussels sprouts, a creamy-looking rice pudding, biscuits and cheese and some russet apples of the kind he most liked.

With a sigh of satisfaction, he drew up a chair and began

to eat. He might die of cold, or of thirst, but he would not die of starvation. The cook who had cooked the meal deserved congratulations and ought not to be brushed aside by Mr. Randall as a cook "of sorts." Cooking of this standard would go a long way towards supplementing the meagre warmth of the Holside Manor fires.

The meal finished, Julian sat on in contentment and repletion. The time went by; there was no sign of Biscoe to clear the table, and presently Julian, with a great yawn, decided that there was nothing to do but get into bed and have a long night's sleep.

He saw with some irritation that there were no facilities in his room for washing; he would have to go into the bathroom to clean his teeth. Sponge-bag in hand, he made the journey along the corridor once more, returning to his room to find that all traces of his meal had been removed and the table folded up and placed in a corner. The fire had gone down, and Julian decided that he would put on to it the remaining half of his coal supply and then lie in bed under the blankets, which he had assured himself were four in number and thick in quality, and watch the leaping flames until he sank into slumber.

He walked to the coal scuttle and, coming to a dead stop beside it, stared at it with an astonishment bordering on stupefaction.

It was empty. There was nothing left in it; nothing whatsoever, he found, bending down and peering into it incredulously. There was nothing, not one lump.

For a few moments, he persuaded himself that he had, on his entrance into the room, thrown on all the coal in an effort to reduce the chill of the room. But . . . no. He was not mistaken, he told himself; he had used half, and half only.

For some reason—ordered, perhaps, by his hospitable master—Biscoe had removed the rest of the coal when bringing in or removing the meal.

Julian backed thoughtfully to the bed and sat on it, staring at the embers and trying to reach a solution of the puzzle. Why, he asked himself, why would Biscoe remove the coal a bare half-hour after having assured him that it had been put there for his use? Why should . . .

It was no use, he decided impatiently. Old Mr. Randall was no doubt mad; Biscoe, for all his wisely-gentle air, was probably mad too. The house was a madhouse and the sooner he got out of it, the happier he would be. For the present, he would get into bed before the chill worked through to his very bones.

He took off his dressing gown, drew back the bed covers and stood once more transfixed. The blankets, which he had inspected, which he had counted, which he had weighed, were gone. Fleece and thickness had vanished; nothing was left but two miserable and threadbare coverings.

Anger, slow, unaccustomed and shaking, welled up in Julian. Without pausing further to look for reasons, he flung on his dressing gown and, striding to the door, threw it open and marched down the corridor. They could play ghosts and brownies and polter-those-things if they cared to, but he was not going to be subjected to treatment of this kind. He was going downstairs to find the butler; if he could not find the butler, he would seek out and find Mr. Randall; he would inform him that someone else might come and value his pictures; he, Julian Rowland Had-for-a-Sucker Hurst was leaving in the morning—and in the meantime, he would have blankets and he would have coal.

Striding purposefully down the corridor, Julian found that

he was going in the wrong direction; he had passed the bathroom and was going away from the staircase up which Biscoe had led him earlier in the evening. Swinging about angrily, he was about to march in the opposite direction, when he found himself outside the room which he had seen when going to have his bath. He was passing the door—he had almost passed it—when what he saw within the room brought him up short. He looked, and one glance was enough. The fire which had been dim was now a roaring blaze; the bed bulged with heavy coverings. A coal scuttle stood, not empty, but almost full of large lumps of incipient heat and cheer.

Without hesitation, he pushed the door open further and strode into the room. For a moment he stood blinking in the firelight, and then an exclamation made him turn towards the hearth, upon which a bundle seemed to be stirring. Taking a step forward, Julian found himself staring down at a girl who, even in his rage, he saw to be one who was warm and comfortable, whose cheeks were flushed with warmth from the leaping fire, whose bare toes wriggled in content and comfort, whose dressing gown was open from excess of warmth, whose entire appearance proclaimed her to be basking, to be immune from the chill and cheerlessness of the house and impervious to the discomfort of those living in it.

"Well, I'm damned!" brought out Julian, slowly.

"That door," said the girl. "It won't shut properly."

He scarcely heard her. He was advancing towards the fire and, without further speech but with an expression which left her in no doubt of his feelings, picked up the coal scuttle.

"Mine, I think," ·he said, and walked towards the bed. "And my blankets, I'm pretty certain—ah! I thought so. If you *don't* mind, I'll—"

43

"Oh, no!" begged the girl, in an anguished voice. "You couldn't—you couldn't be so mean!"

Julian, putting down the coal scuttle, prepared to strip the blankets off the bed.

"Four, if I remember," he said.

"Do you want me to freeze?" she cried.

"Yes. And slowly," said Julian. He paused and turned to look at her. "You took them off my bed, didn't you?"

"Well, yes, in a way, I did," she admitted.

"And you took my coal."

"I won't say I didn't," she said cautiously. "But there were only two on my bed, not warm ones like yours, but two dreadful ones with no fluff on them and—"

"I've seen them," pointed out Julian coldly. "They're on the bed in my room—where you put them."

She was still on the hearthrug, but she had turned from the fire and was sitting back on her heels and looking up at him.

"I'm sorry," she said.

"What did you think I was going to do all night?" demanded Julian. "Lie there shivering?"

"I saw you when you arrived," said the girl. "I looked over the banisters when Biscoe was bringing you up. I wanted to see if you were the type who'd feel the cold, and I saw that you weren't."

"I'm the type that feels it very much," Julian informed her. "You can go and snatch Mr. Randall's blankets. You're not going to have mine."

"If that beastly lock on the door hadn't been loose," she said, "you'd never have found out."

"I was on my way downstairs to kick up a howling row. I suppose you thought I looked the type that couldn't count."

44

"Look," she said, with an air of reasonableness, "can't we go halves?"

"We can. You can have your blankets and I'll have mine."

"You see," she said, "you've got an unfair advantage. You were given the good blankets and the extra coal because you were a visitor."

"Well, aren't you a visitor, too?" enquired Julian.

"No. I'm the staff," she replied.

"Staff?" Julian stared at her incredulously. "Staff?"

"I'm the cook," she said. "Or rather, I'm the cook-house-keeper. Or more accurately, I'm the cook-housekeeper parlourmaid housemaid scullery maid boots and general runaround. I cooked your dinner. I brought it up to your room. I carried up the full dishes because I'm young and strong, and Biscoe took the empty ones down because he's old and feeble. I got your room ready. I made your bed— all those thick, fat blankets because you were a visitor. I wouldn't have put them all on, but I knew Biscoe would count them. I gave you a nice meal to keep you warm all night; now you owe me those blankets and that coal to keep me warm all night. You see?"

He looked at her. Her hair was soft and dark; her skin was clear and looked golden in the firelight; her eyes were blue. Her nose was small and undistinguished, but her mouth was beautiful; Julian's eyes came to rest on it and he found himself sinking into a mood of delightful speculation.

"Are you listening to me?" she asked at last, with a frown.

"On and off. Where were we?" he asked.

"I told you I was the cook—did you hear up to there?"

"I heard, but I didn't believe it. You don't look like a cook and you don't sound like a cook."

"But I cook like one."

45

"Yes, you do. My name's Julian Hurst, by the way. What's yours?"

"Alexandra Bell. You're here to go through all that stack of pictures in the North Room, aren't you?"

"Yes." He walked towards the fireplace, and she moved to make room for him. "Are you really the cook-housekeeper and so on and so on?" he asked.

"Yes. Temporary. The regular one's away and I'm here for a fortnight or thereabouts. Look, if you'd let me have some more coal to pile on the fire, it might keep most of the night."

"If you're on the staff, why on earth can't you get as much coal as you want? You can find your way to the coal house, I presume, and as you're young and strong—you said—you could carry it up here and be nice and warm—no?"

"If I could get anything—coal or anything else—in this house," said Alexandra, "would I be sleeping under those miserable blankets? There's an impregnable combination here: Mr. Randall's a miser—a real miser, in the Scrooge tradition—and his butler, Biscoe, is the most honest old servant alive. He's longing to give me all the blankets I want, but he says that he's Mr. Randall's servant and that he's bound to do as he wants him to. He says that he's given a strict allowance of everything and has to stick to it. So he sticks to it. So I go without my blankets and so I take yours. What would you have done in my place?"

"Exactly as you did. What would you do in mine?"

They looked at one another, and their laughter rang out and filled the far corners of the shadowy room. Presently she sobered and, with an easy, uncoiling movement, rose to her feet.

"You know," she said, "you can't just take the blankets and walk off with them."

"Why not?"

"Because although they're yours, technically, you're a man and you have to give up things for a woman. If you don't feel chivalrous, we could draw lots or something, but there's no way we can *both* be warm, is there?"

He knew one way. He was just going to say so, when he met her glance and the words died unuttered on his lips. He had never seen a cobra about to strike, but this was clearly what it looked like: quiet, motionless and charged with deadly danger.

"Is there?" asked Miss Bell once more, a silky note in her voice.

"I don't think there is," said Julian, and was appalled to hear a sheepish note in his voice. "All right," he went on, "you can keep the coal and I'll take two of the blankets."

She gave him a smile that warmed him, he thought, more than a ton of coal would have done. Armed with the blankets, he obeyed a silent but unmistakable signal that the interview was at an end, and turned towards the door.

"Good night," she said, "and thank you very much. Only . . . I don't see what else you could have done."

"Chivalry and whatnot?"

"No, oh no. Just knowing what's good for you. After all, I *am* the cook, and if you did anything I didn't like, I—"

"—could shove in slow poison. I know." He gave her a slow and irresistible smile. "Good night, Alexandra."

"Miss Bell is much shorter," pointed out Miss Bell.

"Oh . . ." The monosyllable was soft and long drawn-out and lasted until Julian had almost closed the door after him. "Oh . . . I'm not in any hurry, Alexandra. Good night."

Chapter 3

JULIAN WAS WAKENED next morning by the sound of Biscoe bringing in his morning tea and drawing his curtains. He sat up in bed, shuddered at the cold and then forgot his discomfort as his eyes fell upon the view to be seen through the large windows.

The house, as he knew, was built on the shelf of a hill; what he had not realized on the previous evening was the steepness with which the road climbed and the height at which the four houses stood. They commanded a magnificent view of the hills round about and the moorland beyond; Holside Manor had, in addition, a round-the-corner glimpse of the valley.

The lovely country, the shafts of sunlight, raised Julian's spirits to cheerfulness, and the memory of his meeting with Alexandra Bell on the previous night added the last touch of felicity to his mood. A girl . . . What a Godsend she was going to be, he mused, sitting up in bed and tucking the blankets well down behind him in order to be warm while he drank his tea. A girl, praise be. On his arrival at the house, the prospect of working in it for even a day had been a dread one. Now the gloom had vanished and the immediate future was full of delightful possibilities.

Alexandra Bell. Odd sort of job for that sort of girl, but all sorts of girls did all sorts of jobs nowadays. Pretty? Oh, much more than pretty; she was a beauty. Age? Round about twenty-two; more, judging by the ease with which she had X-rayed the sheep's clothing. Alexandra . . . It suited her; a difficult name to carry off, as it were, but it sat well upon her.

Julian got out of bed, performed his shaving and dressing in the shortest possible time, and was ready to go downstairs when Biscoe knocked on the door and came into the room.

"Will you have your breakfast up here, sir?" he asked. "Mr. Randall said—"

"Not here, no," said Julian. "I'll have it in the North Room, if you'll show me where that is."

He followed the old man downstairs and across the hall into what appeared to be a separate wing, and Julian was glad to find that he would be working well out of sight and sound of his host. Biscoe opened the door of a room and Julian, going in, found himself in a large, square apartment looking out on to a lawn.

He looked about him and saw, without surprise, that the amount of work in front of him was considerable, and quite out of proportion to the fee that Mr. Randall had offered. There were pictures all round the room; they stood in rows on the floor, upon tables and chairs or any piece of furniture which could accommodate them. Their frames ranged from plain modern ones to elaborate old gilt ones, and the subjects and sizes of the pictures were as varied as their frames.

In the middle of the room some sort of clearing had been made and chairs and a table placed for Julian's use. Here Biscoe, returning with a loaded tray, laid breakfast, and Julian left alone to eat it, found the meal as warm and as satisfying as his dinner had been the night before. He ate with relish, lit a cigarette, smoked it leisurely and then, rising, picked up the tray, opened the door by a complicated system involving one hand and one foot, walked into the passage and turned in what he thought to be the direction of the kitchen.

He found it without difficulty; it proved to be as large as the size of the house had led him to expect, but it was warm. Compared with the other rooms he had been in, it was almost snug, and in it, trim and neat in a white overall, Alexandra Bell was working.

She looked up as he entered, and stood watching silently as he manoeuvred his tray through the door and put it on to the table.

"Breakfast dishes, empty," he announced. "Good morning, Alexandra. You slept warmly, I trust?"

"Good morning. I slept very well," she said. "Will you come in here for coffee at eleven, or shall I send it in to you?"

"Guess," invited Julian, sitting down at the table and holding out his cigarette case.

"No, thank you," said Alexandra. "I don't smoke, and even if I did, I wouldn't while I'm in the middle of preparing a meal."

He smiled up at her.

"Don't stand there," he begged. "I shall have to get up again."

"You'll have to do that anyway," she told him. "You're working in the North Room."

"Presently, presently," he said. "I'm just trying to get properly acquainted, that's all."

She looked down at him with a slight smile, but her voice was firm.

"Eleven prompt," she said. "And don't light that cigarette —go and enjoy it in the North Room."

"All right." He rose obediently. "Eleven o'clock."

He was back at five minutes to eleven and, this time, he lit a cigarette leisurely, sat on a high-backed wooden chair and studied her frankly.

She was smaller than she had looked in the firelight, but she was slender and long-legged. She had a low voice and her way of speaking was unhurried. Some of the things she said, Julian thought, might almost have been uttered by his aunt Rowena, but there was nothing sardonic about Alexandra. She brought out her frankest speeches without emphasis, and he had sometimes to look at her expression in order to find a clue to her meaning. Her expression, however, helped him very little. In her eyes lurked something—amusement, he would have thought, if he had cared to admit that she seemed to find him amusing—not as other girls had found him amusing, but in a new and disconcerting way, a way that was vaguely disquieting. Nobody had ever laughed at him before.

She poured out his coffee and her own and set the coffee pot between them.

"Before you drink that," she said, "Biscoe thinks you'd better bring in all those things you left in your car. They were all right there for one night, but he'd feel happier if they were indoors. He would have brought them in, but I told him you'd prefer to do it yourself."

51

Julian went out to the garage and carried in his second suitcase and the rest of his equipment. Alexandra looked at the latter with wide eyes as he carried it through the kitchen and into the hall, and was still looking thoughtful when he returned from putting everything upstairs in his room.

"There you are, that's done," he said, sitting opposite to her once more.

"There was a lot of it," she commented. "Did you forget your toboggan?"

"Where I'm going," Julian told her, "toboggans are provided."

"I see. And a nice mountain to toboggan down, I hope?"

"Everything. I'm going up to Scotland to stay with my godmother."

"Ah, the address on the labels. Blairwhinnie Castle."

"That's it. She lives there."

"My godmother lives in a castle," murmured Alexandra, stirring her coffee. "That would make a nice beginning to a rhyme, wouldn't it?

> My godmother lives in a castle,
> With sporrans and tartans and kilts,
> And bagpipes and haggis and oatcakes
> And . . ."

"And claymores with fine jewelled hilts," finished Julian. "How's that?"

"It'll do. Is it a nice castle or a mouldering one?"

"Both the castle and my godmother are very well preserved. I'll take you up there and show them to you one day."

"That's very kind of you," said Alexandra, "but I'd like to remind you that getting into castles, nowadays, is almost easier for me than for you. Your godmother may be an exception, of course, but the normal castle-dweller doesn't really welcome visitors as warmly as he or she once did. Visitors might even be frowned upon, but a cook . . . when a cook comes into sight, the drawbridge goes down and the flag goes up. It's very gratifying."

"Alexandra—" he began impulsively.

"Well?"

"You haven't always—I mean, have you always been a—a cook?"

"No. Only off and on," said Alexandra. "I can do several other things equally well. Can you?"

"I can paint. And—well—"

"And ski, and skate," prompted Alexandra encouragingly. "Is this party at the castle going to be a nice one?"

"Very nice, and put on more or less specially for me. I thought that after a week or so of Mr. Randall and his pictures, I'd need a pick-me-up—and look how wrong I was. Alexandra, please will you tell me all about yourself?"

"It won't take long," she said, in her calm way. "Born in London, brought up in London, went to school in London, parents died in London—father when I was three, mother when I was sixteen. Since then I've been earning my own living. And now nearly twenty-three, unwed, but tremendously sought after. That's all to date." She put her elbows on the table, rested her chin on her hands and looked across at him with an expression of rapt interest. "Now *dooo* tell me about yourself, Mr. Hurst."

"You really want to know?"

"No, but this coffee's too hot to drink."

"Well, as you insist. You know, we've got a lot in common. I was born in London, too; we've got a house up on

53

Campden Hill. I'll show it to you when we get back to town —if you're going back. How long are you going to be here?"

"Not long. When the regular cook comes back, I'll go."

"Go where?"

"To London, to another job."

"Another job like this one?"

"When you're earning your own living," said Alexandra, "that is, really earning your bread on the no-job, no-eat system, you don't worry overmuch about what particular job, and where. You don't spend weeks in between jobs, waiting for something nice and easy to turn up. You take what comes, and the pay that goes with it. Now you've got to drink up your coffee and go back to your job."

Julian looked at her with knitted brows.

"What's the matter with you?" he asked. "Here we are, the only two really living creatures in this house and you— Why can't you behave as though you're glad to have me here? I'm damn glad to have you. Before I saw you last night, I was going to chuck the job back in old Randall's face, but you've—well, you've spread a sort of rosy glow over the prospect. And there's another thing: this kitchen's nice and warm, and I'm going to spend a lot of time in it. If you think I'm in the way, I'm even prepared to do one or two not-too-menial jobs, but you can't expect me to stay in that junk room all the time."

"If the pictures were all junk, you wouldn't be here," said Alexandra.

"I haven't really made a start yet, but I'm not expecting to find much. All Randall really wants me to do is to look out for the work of an artist called Clauval, who was a fellow who seems to have painted some of his pictures with his right hand, and the rest with his feet. The good stuff is having, or is about to have, a mild sort of vogue, and Randall doesn't want to miss any profit that might be going."

"Well, why don't you go and start?"

"Can I have my meals in here?"

She hesitated.

"It would save a lot of carrying," she said at last. "But you'll have to be punctual. Breakfast at nine, coffee at eleven, lunch at one, tea at four and dinner at half-past seven. Biscoe has his an hour earlier and then takes in Mr. Randall's."

Julian was more than punctual; he arrived well before the meals and stayed long after them and Alexandra, having made it clear that she preferred to have the kitchen to herself, went on with her work and occasionally gave him something to do, in order to keep his hands, she said, as busy as his tongue.

Julian was happier than he would have thought possible. Attempting to put his finger on the exact reason for his contentment, he felt that it went deeper than the fact that there was a girl in the house, and a pretty one. Any reasonably attractive girl would have helped to pass the time pleasantly, but Alexandra, he felt, even at this early stage of their acquaintance, was a good deal more than reasonably attractive. He knew a great many girls as pretty; he knew efficient girls and amusing girls and girls with lovely figures, but he knew no girl who combined all these qualities in her own person and added something more, something he could not name, but which he thought his father would have called style. She was a cook; after her first comments on the fact, she had not spoken of it again; she elaborated nothing, explained nothing; she made no attempt to help him to bridge the gaps in his knowledge or estimate of her. He could accept her as she was, and put her story together as best he might—and always he seemed to detect her faint air of enjoying a mild joke at his expense. She fended off skilfully his attempts at getting to know her better, and soon he fell back on his own observation, and began to understand something of her impish humour, her smiling acceptance of conditions which most girls of his acquaintance would have thought insupportable. She had to work hard, and for long hours; she had little free time, and nothing to help her to spend it amusingly. Her clothes looked well on her, but he knew that they had no real warmth. In spite of all this, she had, more than anyone he had ever met, an air of well-being.

She was, up to a point, friendly, and she answered his questions with apparent fullness and frankness; it was only when Julian was back in the North Room, with leisure to go over their conversation, that he realized how much she could say without saying anything.

He learned very little about the master of the house, and was not sufficiently interested to find out more. Biscoe came and went—hardworking, gentle and invariably silent. Alexandra did what she could to help him, and made Julian do more; Biscoe merely smiled his thanks and went on with his task of looking after his master, but sometimes there would be a soft knock on the door of the North Room and he would come in and stand quietly watching Julian as he turned over picture after picture, examined each one, entered it on the growing list and placed it among the orderly procession of those already dealt with. One room had been insufficient for his needs, and he and Biscoe together opened the wide doors leading to the rooms on either side of the North Room, and this extra length, while doing nothing to raise the temperature in which he worked, gave Julian space and freedom and even exercise.

His outdoor exercise was taken in company with Alexandra.

Having discovered that a cook was unable to leave her kitchen in order to accompany him whenever he felt inclined to go out, Julian produced a sheet of paper and wrote on it a schedule of her day's duties. Her free time he marked in red, encircling it with a series of drawings illustrating winter sport in all forms. Their exercise, however, took the form of walks—long, happy walks up and down hills and over the open moors. They went down, sometimes, into the village and made friends with stout Mrs. Cole, of the Rose & Crown and were privileged to be invited into her cozy parlour behind the public bar, and sample her homemade parsnip wine. When they tired of walking, they drove for miles around the lovely countryside, and then Alexandra waited for him while he put the car in the garage, and they would hurry across the yard and seek the warmth of the kitchen.

Warmth. . . . Julian had never appreciated warmth before. His home, his school, his shop—he had never felt cold in any of them. Out of doors, his warm clothing was of good quality, his shoes stout and his gloves fur-lined. He bought them, wore them and was warm. But up here at Holside, in a house with large rooms, wide, draughty corridors and a minimum of heating, he found that warmth did not come easily; it had to be won. He was wearing the thickest clothes he had brought with him, but he would have given a great deal for a supply of the kind of underwear he had seen worn by Mr. Randall on the night of his arrival. His opinion of long woollen underpants had gone from scorn to respect and from respect to longing. When he was out of doors, he could discard most of his heavy clothing and bring a glow to his body by exercise, but the glow was dimmed by the knowledge that Alexandra's coat kept out no cold and her shoes no moisture. They looked sensible, but he knew that the materials of which they were made were far from hard-wearing. He was ashamed of his own warm coat and gloves, of the comfort and dependability of his footwear. He watched her anxiously in the bitter wind, expecting her to grow wan and pinched, and saw that she was rosy and bright-eyed. She allowed him to draw her hand into the warm depths of his pocket, and so they walked. It seemed to him that nothing could depress her; she was quiet, but always, in her eyes, was the faint look of amusement, as though she was smiling at the oddities of life. There was an elusive quality about her that he was beginning to fear, and he was glad to feel her hand in his; it was something he could hold on to, something that linked them.

"It's good air." Alexandra sniffed it appreciatively at the end of a steep climb. "But there's an awful lot of it. I wonder how I'd like to live here permanently?"

"Not *here!*"

"Why not here? Holside's a lovely place, and the house could be made nice and friendly—it's only Mr. Randall that gives it that bleak feeling. But I don't think that Londoners, born and bred Londoners like me, ever do more than think that they *ought* perhaps to live in the country. I get waves of self-reproach sometimes because I feel that I ought to be missing all those things that sound so beautiful in poems—green fields and leafy lanes and the song of birds. Do you ever say to yourself, 'I must get out of this city and *grow*'?"

"Never."

"Neither do I."

"Then that's settled that. Tell me, why were you called Alexandra?"

"Father's mother. Where does Julian come from?"

"Mother's father. She admits now that it was a mistake,

58

but she said that when she first murmured it over my downy head, she thought it had a vaguely patrician sound. I can't really escape it, because my only other name is Rowland, after a godfather who had the bad taste to leave all his money away from me. You can't say that Roly's any improvement on Julian, can you? And besides, I—"

"Look! A robin!"

"Do you mean that you weren't even listening to what I was saying?"

"I wasn't *not* listening."

"If all you need," said Julian, "is background music, then I really think—"

"Look! It's skipping!"

"That, my dear Alexandra, is called hopping, and it isn't a robin. Look, you're not going back already, are you? We've got lots of time."

"You have; I've got to go back and do some work."

"What gives you this idea that I'm a drone?" he asked, as they turned in the direction of home. "I run a business. Correction: I run half a business, but the business is quite sound and I'm on the job most of the time. This job of old Randall's is outside my line, and I was only pushed into it by my father and my brother."

"What inducements did they use?"

"What pushed the scales down," admitted Julian, "was the chance of going up and doing a bit of skiing in Scotland. Anybody can go and ski in Scotland, of course, but not everybody can do it in the comfort provided by my dear godmamma."

"When's the party?"

"I gave myself ten days here."

"Ten days? This job won't take you ten days!"

59

He smiled at her.

"This job," he said, "will take as long as I want it to take. Mr. Randall isn't concerned about time. The fee's a fixed one, if you call it a fee. If he pays you at the same rate as he pays me, you're not going to make your fortune here."

"Wise people," said Alexandra, "don't underpay good cooks. Have you found any of the pictures Mr. Randall brought you here to find?"

"The Clauvals? I've found two."

"Are they good?"

"Do you know anything about pictures?"

"Not much."

"Then it's no use talking technicalities to you. But they're not good. They're bad. In fact, they're terrible. It doesn't seem possible that anybody could turn out work that varied as much as this fellow's does."

"Can I look at them?"

"Of course, you can look at them whenever you like. If you've got no eye, they won't distress you, but whichever way you look at them, you'll find them bad. They're genuine Clauvals, though."

"Why do you sell pictures instead of painting pictures?" asked Alexandra. "Did you paint bad ones, like Clauval?"

"Certainly not. It was my aunt's idea. She put up most of the money, and so we're in business."

"Do you like it? Yes," she answered herself, "you do like it, or you wouldn't be doing it. You wouldn't do anything unless it amused you."

"Is that an assessment of my character?"

"I'm not sure that you've got much character," said Alexandra judicially. "I'm not criticizing; I'm just stating a fact. Some people have to go through life working at something, and some people, like you, just have to go through life. The first time I heard you speak, I heard a clicking sound."

"A—?"

"The silver spoon," said Alexandra. "The sound is unmistakable. Whenever I hear it, I tell myself not to expect too much."

"My character is—"

"You can do without one," said Alexandra. "Cooks have to have characters, but you can get along very well as you are."

"Thank you. Thank you very much, Miss Bell. Would you like my opinion of your character?"

"Not now; we're nearly home, if that's the right word."

"It's a funny thing," said Julian, "but I haven't walked—straight walks like these, I mean—since I was dragged out at my prep school. I'm rather enjoying it."

"That," concluded Alexandra, after reflection, "must be due to my company. I like walking. I walk round the city on Sundays, when it's nice and empty. I look at the Mansion House, and I go round St. Paul's and—"

"Tell me something," asked Julian. "How much spare time does a cook have for things like wooing or being wooed?"

"I'll think it over while I'm peeling the potatoes," said Alexandra.

Back in the North Room, he worked with his mind on the night of his first meeting with Alexandra, and realized how far he had travelled since then. He had told her that he was not in a hurry, and he had already discovered that the words were not true. He was impatient and restless and he wanted to reach a point in their relationship beyond their present easy companionship. There was another Alexandra somewhere; he glimpsed her now and then, but he could not

61

reach her. The lovely mouth smiled at him, the blue eyes looked into his with seeming candour, but there was something—he could not tell what—in their depths. Somewhere, eluding him, was the other Alexandra, and he sensed that it was the real Alexandra. He wanted the real Alexandra. He wanted her passionately, and he wanted her in a hurry.

And something told him that, for the first time in his life, he was not going to get what he wanted.

Chapter 4

AT THE END of his fifth day at Holside, Julian acknowledged to himself, soberly, and with a great deal of reluctance, that he liked Alexandra Bell more than he had ever liked a girl before.

The conclusion was a disturbing one. Members of his family had more than once taken him to account for knowing too many girls, or for knowing them too well; in the course of a discussion on the topic with his mother, he remembered having told her, with some sharpness, that he had his emotions well in hand. He wished very much that he could say the same now, but his emotions, far from being in hand, were galloping with frightening speed and taking him to the point at which he realized that he was going to ask Alexandra to marry him.

He knew that, if she agreed, she would be received by his family with relief and pleasure; some of his preliminary skirmishes had given them cause for a good deal of apprehension. On the subject of Alexandra's feelings, he was in the dark, and likely to remain so until he declared himself openly and unequivocally; she was as cool as on the evening they had first met, and there was a light in her eye that told him that she was following with perfect ease and not a little amusement, the progress of his passion. There were, he acknowledged ruefully to himself, no flies on Alexandra.

His feeling for her shook him. It was in vain that he reminded himself, again and again, that she was only a girl; the reminder did nothing to reduce his mounting temperature. Falling back upon common sense, he argued that they were shut up here together, he and she, and it was only natural that . . . But if it was so natural, why was Alexandra so cool and so unmoved? There were times when, fantastic though it seemed, he thought that she was laughing at him. She treated him kindly, she gave him all her free time; last night, when they parted at the door of her room, she had watched him as he bent closer and had done nothing to evade the light kiss he had placed on her lips. She treated the whole affair, he thought with rising anger, as though it were some sort of game that they had both played many times, a game which enlivened these dull winter days but which they would cease to play when other diversions offered.

He might, in another circumstance, have considered the alternative of testing the strength of his feelings by a policy of avoidance, but as they were situated, this was impossible. He was bound to be in her company day after day; short of giving up his work in the North Room and returning to London and the safety of numbers, he must go on seeing her, passing enchanted hours with her.

Common sense fled. He remembered dimly that he had

64

once made a resolution—a resolution that had all the fervour of a vow—that he would not marry until he was thirty. Three more years . . . three years without Alexandra. . . . He shuddered, put the memory from him and gave himself up to dreams.

The five days became a week, and then two events occurred which made Julian a happy man: Alexandra kissed him, for the first time, as though she meant it, and he found four pictures representing Clauval's best work.

Four pictures. He came upon them at the end of a long and somewhat tedious day's work. They were almost the last of Mr. Randall's collection, and they proved to be the last Clauvals. Four—but they were four pictures which gave Julian a feeling of amazed delight and roused him to the keenest professional enthusiasm.

He carried them, one by one, across the room and placed them in a good light. They were all of the same subject, the head of a young girl; only the background differed, being in each case painted in a different colour. A pencilled note behind each picture named them: *Green Girl, Blue Girl, Gold Girl, Silver Girl.* They were all the same size; they were not large, the girl was not beautiful and the pose in each case left something to be desired, but the work was exquisite, and Julian looked at them with a double interest: that of the artist and that of the dealer.

He was still looking at them when the door opened; he turned his head, hoping to see Alexandra, but it was Biscoe who came in, carrying the week's newspapers which Mr. Randall, having read, had passed on to his guest.

"I don't want those, thank you," said Julian. "You can take them away—but first, come here and look at these."

Biscoe understood both gestures: repudiation and invitation.

He came over and stood beside Julian, and together they looked at the four pictures.

"What I can't understand, and what no other artist can understand, is how the devil this Clauval could have had two utterly separate techniques. It's all the one Clauval; there isn't any doubt about that, because even in his worst pictures there's a line, a touch here and there, that stands out and identifies him. But these four pictures show you what he could do when he was really trying." Biscoe could not follow, but Julian was pursuing his own train of thought. "*This* Clauval was a—"

Chancing to look at Biscoe, the words died on his lips and he remained staring in stupefaction. Rolling, slowly but steadily, down the old man's cheeks was a trickle of tears.

Julian had often seen tears on Biscoe's cheeks. His eyes watered when he went outside to fetch coal, or when he stoked the fire or when he opened one of the windows and cold air blew in upon him. There was, indeed, at most times a suggestion of glistening in his eyes. But Julian was aware that he was looking now at real and deep grief. The old man's shoulders were shaking and, though he made no sound, it was plain that he was almost unbearably affected.

Julian waited for a few moments and then, putting a hand on the servant's thin shoulder, guided him to a chair and pressed him on to it. Biscoe, with a tremulous shake of the head, stood up again immediately and, fishing a large handkerchief from his pocket, wiped his eyes, blew his nose and looked up at Julian in a shamefaced manner.

"I'm sorry, sir. That was very foolish of me. But the pictures . . . they—they took me without warning, sir. I haven't seen them for over twenty years."

66

"Where did Mr. Randall buy them, do you know?" asked Julian.

He had to repeat the question twice before Biscoe understood it. Then the old man looked surprised.

"He didn't buy them, sir," he said. "They were painted in the house—in Mr. Randall's house in Devonshire, where he lived before he came up here, sir."

Julian stared at him, too astounded for speech. Biscoe looked back at him and a worried frown appeared on his forehead.

"I thought Mr. Randall would have told you, sir," he faltered. "Perhaps I shouldn't have said anything."

Julian hesitated. He was, he felt certain, on the verge of some knowledge which went beyond Mr. Randall's concerns, a discovery of interest to those who had sought, unsuccessfully, for a solution to the mystery of Clauval and his work. The possibility that Mr. Randall had at one time commissioned the artist had not once occurred to him, and he regretted the casual way in which he had inferred that nothing but cupidity lay behind the decision to catalogue the collection of pictures.

He picked up one of the Clauvals and held it up between his hands.

"When were these pictures painted?" he asked quietly. The tone of his voice, he knew, would make no difference to Biscoe, but he wanted to give an impression that he was not unduly interested in the matter.

"They were painted just before we left the other house, sir," said Biscoe, a little unsteadily. "But Mr. Randall . . . if he didn't say anything to you, Mr. Hurst, sir, then I—"

"Do you know who the girl in the picture is?" asked Julian.

"Oh yes, sir!" Biscoe seemed to hesitate, and the next

words came out with a rush. "That's Mr. Randall's daughter, sir."

Without waiting to say more, Biscoe turned and went with shuffling but determined steps to the door. His demeanour was that of a man who has said too much and is resolved to say not a word more. The door closed behind him and Julian, after putting the pictures carefully aside, went swiftly to find Alexandra and tell her the news.

"I've learned something," he announced, going into the kitchen and beginning his story before the door had closed behind him. "Something about Clauval."

She turned from the stove and looked at him.

"Well?" she asked.

"It wasn't anything about Clauval, exactly. But I've found some of his good work."

"You *have?* Are you sure?"

"Of course I'm sure. Do you want to come and see them?"

"I'd love to."

They went to the North Room together, and Julian lined up the four pictures for her inspection. She examined them with interest, and then turned to him.

"Are these what Mr. Randall brought you up here to look for?" she asked.

"I imagine so. He obviously knew they were here, but he wanted to be told whether they were good or not. Surprise number one: they were actually painted in his house, not in this house, but in the house he lived in before he came here. Surprise number two: guess who the girl is."

Alexandra turned and looked at the pictures once more.

"I suppose if he had a daughter," she said at last, "this could be it. Her. She."

"Well, you're right. It is it, her, she."

"They're lovely. *Green Girl, Blue Girl, Gold Girl, Silver Girl.* Lovely! How did you find out who she was? Oh—Biscoe!"

"Yes. He let it slip out, and he's sorry; he feels he's said too much, and I'm quite certain he won't say any more. Nor will Mr. Randall, he hints. I'll ask Biscoe where the daughter is, anyway."

He asked, and Biscoe told him, but the information left Julian where he had been before. Mr. Randall's daughter, said Biscoe, had been dead for some years.

"Well, that's that," said Julian to Alexandra. "Well, I'll finish the job and make a report—and I'll make an offer for those four pictures, too."

"What did he say he was going to do with them?"

"I gathered that he'd sell any good Clauvals I found. The rest of the collection, I imagine, will be left as it is, to be sold for what it'll fetch when he's dead."

"What are those four Clauvals worth?"

"Not much at the moment; they're being bought, as you might say, speculatively. If anybody brought one of them into the shop—one of the four we're talking about—I'd buy it for two hundred cash down. Two hundred and ten, if the owners stuck their toes in. They fetch about two hundred and eighty."

"Eighty pounds profit on one little picture?" said Alexandra in astonishment.

"Art dealers have to live," explained Julian. "And remember that I have to split that with Auntie. I'll take you to see her. You'll like her, once you get down to the real it, her, she. And you'll like my mother. She cooks all the time, like you. And you'll like my father; he's got a rather wispy, wistful look and a sagging moustache and he's pining for a

69

girl called Susie Sterndale who worked for him for twenty years and then got swept out of the firm together with a lot of other out-of-date equipment, poor old Susie. I'm not sure what you'll think of my brother or his wife, but their son is a nice, promising fellow, said to be rather like me. He's four and a half and he's called Danny. And I'm going to be made an uncle for the second time when my sister, who's called Drusilla, produces her baby in about two months' time. Alexandra, how many children shall we have . . . one day?"

"I aim to have three," said Alexandra tranquilly. "What about you?"

Julian took three or four steps, slowly and deliberately, and coming to a halt close to her, reached out and drew her gently to him. He held her, looking down at her, studying the face that was in his mind day and night.

"Just stand still," he said softly. "I want to look at you. I want to try and find out what's special about you, what's different. I'd like to try and find out *why* . . . *why* I've fallen in love madly and deeply and, I'm very much afraid, finally in love. Why, Alexandra?"

"Have you fallen in love?"

"Yes. Shall I put it a better way? Alexandra, I love you very much."

She looked at him. Her eyes, blue under dark lashes, were calm; there was a question in them, but it did not appear to be an urgent question. This was not a girl one could rush. She was looking for something, something in his eyes or in his expression. After a time, she smiled, but he could not tell whether she had found what she had looked for. Her smile, her lips close to his own, her gentleness and sweetness drove from him the last remnants of the caution which every night he urged upon himself. Hesitations and doubts fled;

he drew her close, held her to him and put his mouth on hers. When he raised his head, he spoke simply and directly.

"Alexandra, will you marry me?"

She gave a soft exclamation and drew herself out of his arms.

"That was sweet, Julian," she said slowly, "but it was far too early . . . years too early!"

"You mean that just because we've only known—"

"No, oh no! But you said—don't you remember?—that no girl was going to hear those words from you until you were thirty, and—"

"Alexandra, do you love me?" he broke in abruptly.

There was a long pause. The smile left her face and a frown, a small, puzzled frown, appeared on her brow.

"Do you know," she said very slowly, and on a wondering note, "I do. It's odd, isn't it?"

"What's odd about it?" He took one of her hands and held it against his cheek. "What's odd about it, darling? We met, and we fell in love."

"That's all very well as far as it goes," said Alexandra, "but you've left out a lot of important things. We met in an unusual way and we've seen one another for hours every day since then; we've had a clear run, with no competition, and so we've hurried to what you'd call a natural conclusion."

"We're in love—how or why doesn't matter. I can support you, we're both free, and I've asked you to marry me and I'm waiting to hear you say 'Yes' or 'No'."

"Well . . . no," said Alexandra. "Not until we've got back into a world in which there are more than four people—two people. Not until we've thought it out a bit more. You can't lead me to your mother and say, 'Look, Mother, here's a cook I met last week; we're going to be married.' Don't you see?"

"No," said Julian. "Have you ever been in love before?"

"I've been halfway in, once or twice," said Alexandra. "But if romance is going to flower, it's got to have somewhere to flower *in*. Two people who begin to fall in love could often go along very nicely if only they could find somewhere to do their love-making. If it's got off to a good start, as yours and mine did, it'll go along nicely if there's a place, like this kitchen, for instance, where the couple can, so to speak, forgather. But if you'd been living in one room with a gas ring, and if I'd been living in one room with a gas ring, and if it's winter and you can't be out of doors, then it has to be a very strong sort of romance to keep alive and well. If we ever do marry, Julian, do you think we could afford to open a nice, warm, comfortable club where penniless couples can do their wooing?"

"I think we'll keep out of the newspapers," said Julian. "Could you talk to me less and kiss me more? That's nice. Alexandra, when did you first know that you loved me?"

"Not for some time, two days at least. For the first two days I was busy making excuses for you."

"Excuses? What for?"

"For nothing in particular. You were just being you, that's all."

"You'll have a lot of time to get used to that," said Julian. "Forty years at least."

"Can't we just go on as we are until we meet in London?"

"No. I'm going to finish up this job and make my report to old Randall, and then I'm going to show you to my family and keep an eye on you until we're married. Married . . ."

"Does the word frighten you?"

"Yes," admitted Julian frankly, "it does. But I'll get used to it if I keep saying it to myself."

"Supposing I can't get away from here as soon as you can?"

"If old Randall can't get his regular staff back in their regular places in time," said Julian, "then he can do his own cooking. You're coming with me. We— What are you looking at?"

"The clock," said Alexandra. "Oh, Julian, I'll never catch up. Please, darling, go away."

"Can't I help?"

"Yes; go away," said Alexandra.

The following days were, for both of them, full of happiness. The weather was bad, but they scarcely noticed it; they went out in the car when the roads looked clear, and they walked when the snow was too deep for driving. Julian discovered that Alexandra's manner had grown more gay. She had always found a good deal to amuse her, but he had always felt that there was something about her of wariness, of distrust of herself or of him. Now her eyes were unclouded and her mood as light as his own.

When he had finished his work, he asked Biscoe to arrange an interview with Mr. Randall. He was conducted to the room in which he had first seen his host, and found him, as on the previous occasion, sitting squarely in front of the fire and making no attempt to move in order to let Julian share the warmth.

"You've finished?" he asked, in a reedy tone.

"Yes. That's the list," answered Julian, with equal directness. "There are four good Clauvals; I'd like to make you an offer for them."

"How much?" enquired Mr. Randall.

"Two hundred pounds each."

There was a silence, but not a long one.

"No," said Mr. Randall, slowly. "I won't sell to a dealer.

73

If you'll give me that, they must be worth a good deal more. Take them off the list and take them down to your father and tell him I want them put up for auction—Sotheby's. I'll send a cheque to the office for your fee. There's nothing to keep you here any longer, I take it?"

"Nothing."

"Then I'll wish you good day."

Julian bowed, turned and walked out of the room. He found Biscoe waiting for him in the corridor and the two walked together towards the kitchen. Julian smiled down at the old man and Biscoe smiled back a little tremulously.

"You'll be leaving soon, sir?" he asked.

"Tomorrow, Biscoe. I'd like you to give me a hand tonight, packing those four pictures."

"Yes, sir." There was a long pause, and Julian saw that the old man was struggling to say something. He waited, but it was clear that Biscoe had thought better of it. "Yes, sir," he said once more.

The job was done. Nothing remained but to write to his godmother and explain that he was taking Alexandra home in order to show her to his parents as soon as possible; she would give him her blessing and forgive him readily for his failure to keep his engagement.

Engagement . . . For the first time, Julian found himself facing the swiftness with which events had moved since he left Campden Hill. He had come up to Holside with a whole heart; he had been—he fended off the word, but it came back again and again and at last remained—he had been free. He was no longer free, and he had no regrets; he was in love and he knew that Alexandra was the kind of girl his mother, or any mother, dreamed of for her son: a girl of beauty and sweetness and charm. She was his and he was a fortunate

74

man. But . . . love had rushed upon him and enveloped him and smothered him and he felt an urgent need for a breathing space—a brief moment in which to stand between the past and the future to look backward and say good-bye, without regrets, to the old life; to look forward eagerly to the new.

He paced up and down the North Room wondering whether a man in his position might or might not ask for a breathing space. He tried to recall what plans he and Alexandra had made for the immediate future, and could remember nothing but the fact that he was to take her to his home and show her proudly to his family. They had spoken of going to London together, but nothing definite had been fixed upon, nothing decided; their meetings had been too brief, too sweet to be given over to sober planning and exact calculation. They were engaged; she had no ring, but she would have one as soon as he got once more within the sphere of a good jeweller.

He thought of Scotland and had a sudden longing for his godmother's company; she was old and wise and restful, and with her he could pause for a short while and calm his spirit after the tumultuous emotions he had passed through. He rejected without hesitation the idea of taking Alexandra with him; she must meet his mother and father before being presented to any other members of the family circle. And he did not, for this brief interval, want Alexandra with him. Between the past and the future he wanted to build a bridge; when he crossed it, she would be waiting for him. He would explain his feeling to her and she would understand.

He had put off the moment of decision as long as he could, but now with the time of departure near at hand, he tried to put himself in her place and look at the matter from her point of view. He found this more difficult than he had imagined, and so he fell back upon his lifelong habit of arriving at a difficult decision by assessing not how much good he would be doing but how little harm. And viewed in this light, he seemed to be doing very little harm indeed; he was merely carrying out an engagement formed before his meeting with Alexandra, an engagement with his godmother, who was old and to whom he owed a certain duty. No girl could object to his visiting his seventy-year-old godmother; he felt that Alexandra, on the contrary, would give him credit for being considerate—and he would get a short and blessed interval in which to adjust himself to his new circumstances.

The decision was made. In making it, in hearing his own deep sigh of relief, he understood how much had happened in the past few days. He had left London a free man; he was going home to be married, and to be married without undue delay. His iron resolution to remain single until he was thirty had melted in the warmth of Mr. Randall's kitchen. He had given up three years of freedom from responsibility, three years of travel along a path which he now realized was the very one that the poets had dubbed primrose. He had no regrets, he told himself once more, aloud. He was a lucky man to have won Alexandra and he was going to love and cherish her all his life—beginning about a fortnight from now.

It was more difficult to tell her than he had imagined. He rehearsed the very words; he brought them out with exactly the right shade of reasonableness, but they fell from his lips, not the pearls of the fairy story, but of a horrid and unmistakably froggy appearance. But, frogs or pearls, he had brought them into the light, and Alexandra was now examining them with the old gleam suddenly showing in her eyes.

Something was amusing; what, Julian couldn't for the life of him see, but behind her glance was the dancing—he had once thought it a dangerous—light.

"Darling"—The studied casualness had gone from his voice, and he sounded humble and not a little frightened. "Darling, you don't mind, do you?"

Alexandra looked at him with a judicial air, and he felt that he had chosen a bad time to have it out with her. Have what? He checked himself sharply—this was not an issue. But issue or not, a girl rolling out pastry should perhaps not be expected to bring the right amount of seriousness to a discussion of the future.

"Do you, Alexandra?" he asked again.

She leaned over the table and touched his nose lightly with a floury finger, and then leaned back to study the effect.

"You look sweet," she said. "What were you saying? Oh yes, you want time to reflect. Wasn't that it?"

"Alexandra, I—"

"Godmother was the word," said Alexandra, giving him one of her slow, lovely smiles. "But Julian darling, I quite agree that you need time. I asked you, don't you remember? I kept pulling on the reins and saying 'Whoa!' "

"I've gone up to Blairwhinnie, on and off, Alexandra darling, ever since I was—"

"—twelve years old. Julian, what were you like at twelve years old? I'd love to have known you then."

"I was just the same as I am now. I was selfish and low-down and in every way the hound I am today. Alexandra, if you're hurt or—"

"Do I look hurt?" she enquired in astonishment.

He had to admit that she didn't. But—

"Tell me whether I ought to go or not," he urged.

77

"Haven't you got a mind of your own?" said Alexandra, in simple enquiry.

"This conversation," said Julian, "illustrates what I'm feeling, but what I can't express very well. A fortnight ago, Alexandra, I would have had a mind of my own. A fortnight ago, I would have made a decision, right or wrong, and stuck to it."

"Or not stuck to it," put in Alexandra mildly.

"Or not stuck to it. But now I can't have a mind of my own any more. In future, everything I do must be coloured by how it affects somebody else—you. I've got to decide, weigh and then decide again. I've decided that it's right for me . . . correction, that it's all right for me to go up to my godmother's and meet you later on in London. I love you with all my heart, darling, and being away from you even for these few days appalls me, but it gives us both time to get adjusted. We love one another, and we're going to be married. We've got a long life ahead of us, I hope, so what do these few days matter now?"

"What indeed?" recited Alexandra on three blithe notes. "Julian, shall I make this pie with flutey edges with my thumb, like this, or do you prefer them done zing zing zing zing with a knife, like that?"

"For God's sake, Alexandra—"

"Julian, if you're going to your godmother's, I don't think you ought to go God-ing. She won't like it. As your future wife, could I ask whether you have expectations?"

"No expectations," said Julian shortly. "My godparents were extremely ill-chosen. Alexandra, do you mind my going, or don't you?"

"If you mean do I mind *personally*," said Alexandra,

slowly, turning the pie round and inspecting its edges critically, "then the answer is that I don't mind a bit."

"How about impersonally?"

"*Impersonally,* I feel that your godmother could perhaps have survived the shock of being put off. On the other hand, perhaps a fragile old lady hasn't such tough fibres as a quite new and untried fiancée, and when a man feels an instinct to swim to shore and feel some solid ground under his feet— Mind, darling, I want to get this into the oven. Kiss me, Julian."

He went behind her and took her, pie and all, into his arms for a long moment.

"I'm a selfish pig," he murmured.

"Yes," agreed Alexandra.

"Do you love me, selfish pig or not?"

"Yes," said Alexandra.

Julian kissed her with his heart full of gratitude. It was over. He was in love, he was engaged, he was going to be married—but for a few, a very few days, and for the last time, he was his own man. Life was very good and Alexandra . . . Alexandra was the loveliest as well as the most understanding of women.

There was nothing to do now but complete the arrangements for his departure. He was grateful to Alexandra for her tenderness and for her gaiety; she made no further reference to his visit to Scotland; she helped him to pack and had a sensible suggestion to make regarding the four pictures.

"You don't want to take the Clauvals up to Scotland with you, do you?" she asked. "Why don't you let me take them? I shall be going by train and I can keep an eye on them."

"All right," said Julian. "I'll collect them from you in London. My God, Alexandra, do you know that I haven't even got your address?" He took a small notebook from his pocket and looked at her with pencil poised. "Well?"

"Do you know Pimlico?" she asked.

"Pimlico? Certainly not," said Julian. "Do I have to pollute my address book with Pimlicos?"

"You do. Number 13 Nunn—three N's and not two, as in cloistered women—13 Nunn Road, Pimlico. It's a bit difficult to find."

"Darling"—he put away the notebook, leaned forward and kissed her lightly—"instinct will lead me."

"You have instinct?" asked Alexandra. "I thought that was what women—"

"*Intuition*, my sweet, intuition—the thing that made you realize what a wonderful husband I'd make. Alexandra"— His tone lost its lightness and he gathered her to him in an almost hungry grip—"darling, I can't believe I'm not going to see you for the next few days."

"It'll seem a long time," said Alexandra. "Julian, will you remember something for ever and ever and ever?"

"What, darling?"

"I love you very much. Will you keep that in mind?"

"Always," said Julian.

She stood framed in the great front door as he drove away; he looked back for a last wave and saw her, straight and slender. Two tears had shone in her eyes as he left her, and he had kissed them away before they could brim over.

They brimmed over when the car was out of sight, and Alexandra wiped them away resolutely. She did not come inside at once; cold as was the day, she stood gazing at the gateway through which Julian had driven away, and her gaze had in it something of maternal tenderness. But behind the tenderness was the gleam which Julian had seen so often—a soft, dancing light of amusement. If he could have seen it now, he would have been in no doubt of one thing: though it was a blue light, it spelt danger.

Chapter 5

IT CANNOT BE said that Julian added very much to the gaiety of the party at Blairwhinnie. The company was a small one, selected especially for his entertainment; the men and the girls were all old friends with whom, in previous years, he had enjoyed similar gatherings and who knew him as one of the most stimulating members of the circle. The word could scarcely be applied to him now; though he skied during the day, danced every night, played bridge and joined in party games, he found himself unable to bring his mind to present enjoyments; all his thoughts were at Holside, with Alexandra, and he missed her with an acuteness that brought him an equal amount of pain and astonishment.

A week, which last year would have flashed by and left him wondering at the speed with which it had gone, now separated itself into seven long and separate days, each of which, he told himself, might have been spent with Alexandra—seeing her, hearing her, touching her, holding her in his arms. Seven days. He had robbed them both of seven days; seven multiplied by twenty-four hours— There was no need to work out the sum; he knew exactly the number of hours, for the knowledge was not in his head, but in his heart.

His godmother watched him, at first with astonishment, then with anxiety and at last with understanding. She gave him a week and, seeing him as moody and withdrawn at the end of it as at the beginning, manoeuvred him into a quiet corner, put aside the embroidery upon which she was working, took off her glasses and looked at him with humour and affection.

"Something," she said, "is the matter with you."

Julian gave her a look of mingled apology and misery.

"Yes," he admitted. "Something."

"Love?"

"Yes."

"A nice girl?"

He gave the first really happy laugh she had heard from him since his arrival.

"A cook," he said.

"A lady?" pursued his godmother, unmoved.

"Yes."

"Good for her. Being a cook, I mean. Does she like you?"

"She loves me. We're engaged. It was quick, it was sort of instantaneous, but I know that it's what they call the real thing."

"I wouldn't be surprised," said his godmother, regarding him thoughtfully, "if it were. You look . . . I don't know. More purposeful, I think. Why didn't you bring her to me? Ah! I know—you want to show her to your mother first.

But then, why did you come at all? That is, if you could have stayed with her?"

He hesitated, and then felt the need for honesty.

"I came up chiefly for a—a sort of breathing space," he said. "I felt . . . well, I suppose there was a touch of panic somewhere. But now it's more than a touch—now it's a full-scale panic, and for an entirely different reason. I wake up at night sweating because I know I shouldn't have come. I feel . . . I can't quite describe it."

"This breathing space," said his godmother, taking up her work and unfolding it thoughtfully. "Did you tell her about that, or didn't you have to tell her? If she was intelligent, she would have guessed."

"She's very intelligent."

"Did she oppose the idea of your coming here?"

"No. She was wonderful."

He found the grey, wise old eyes raised to his with what he saw, to his astonishment, was a look of worry.

"She—? *What* did you say, Julian, my dear?"

"I said she didn't mind."

"She—" His godmother took off her glasses once more and polished them absently. "Oh dear, oh dear, oh dear," she said softly. "Oh, my poor, poor Julian!"

"Poor?" There was a loud singing in his ears as he waited for her to explain something that had lain at the back of his mind for the past week, vague, dark, threatening. "Poor?"

"Tell me"—His godmother's voice came to him as from a great distance—"tell me, was there anyone else she was in love with before she met you?"

"Anyone else? No." He cleared the hoarseness from his throat. "No. Why?"

84

"Was she absolutely sure that you were the person for her?"

"Ab-absolutely sure. Why?"

"It was only— You see, Julian, your coming up here to survey the situation was a very fine idea from one point of view, your own, but it does seem to me that for a girl of spirit—and a girl who goes out and does a job of work like cooking must have some spirit—she took the whole thing remarkably calmly. When a woman of spirit and intelligence says nothing and allows a man to play a selfish trick on—"

"Selfish?" croaked Julian.

"Mean and thoughtless, I meant. But if she took it quietly, it can mean only one thing, that she—"

"If you'll forgive me," broke in Julian, "I think I could get off before dark and—"

"Don't drive too recklessly," said his godmother. "The roads are very treacherous."

The roads were more than treacherous. Winter, which up to now had been in sportive mood, noticed an expensive car setting out from the Aviemore district, and set itself to the task of showing the driver that the seventh of March, especially in Scotland, was the seventh of March and not the middle of June. Anybody who thought that a powerful engine was a sufficient shield against winter conditions, simply didn't know what winter was capable of, and would have to be shown at once. Winter in London was a gentlemanly fellow, bowler-hatted and carrying an umbrella, but let nobody suppose that he would meet him near Aviemore in March. Far from it. This insolent Londoner in his absurd little long-nosed vehicle would have to be taught to recognize and have a wholesome respect for winter in a tam-o'-Shanter and a plaid. Aye, he would. Aviemore? Och aye, let him

85

go through Aviemore. He'd be making for Pitlochry, the puir laddie. Ho, ho, ho! look at him, slowing down already. Aye, laddie, snow it is, and mair to come. Now on you go; that's it, keep at it, now. Look at that; Kingussie already—why, you're a'most there, mon! London's just round the corner, ho, ho, ho! What's holding you up, laddie? Och now, ye'll do fine if ye can get as far as Dalwhinnie and over the Pass of Drumochter. What's a small matter of two thousand feet on a nice road like this, specially built for ye by General Wade himself. Can't do it? Och, now, come on. Stuck? Ho, ho, ho, ho, ho! Now look at yon hefty Scotsmen gettin' their shoulders behind it and pushing . . . that's right; ye'll have to turn and go back. Ho, ho, ho! Sorry, I canna help blowing. Now . . . a nice bit of mist and a nice, invigorating wind, straight through you and oot the ither side. Sleet and snow and—let me see—some thick ice. Ye'll find it cold up in Inverness, but it's the only way for ye now, back the way ye came, and then down to Fort William. Magnificent scenery, Mr. Hurst, if only ye could see it. Ho, ho, ho! This is Scotland, mind ye, Scotland. Ye're no' in Hyde Park; we keep weather up here, fine, hardening weather, and next time, ye'll remember . . .

Julian never forgot. It was a nightmare journey of three nights and two days. Reason told him to take it in easy stages. Instinct told him that he was driving in pursuit of his life's happiness. He was frightened—of what, he could not have said; all he was certain of was the fact that once he set eyes upon Alexandra once more, his spirit would be calmed.

He got to Campden Hill early on a raw, bleak morning and entered the hall just as his mother was coming down-stairs to prepare breakfast.

"Why, Julian!" she exclaimed. "What a time to arrive! Have you been driving all night?"

"Yes," said Julian, "Hello, Mother."

She looked at his white, drawn face and refrained from asking any of the questions that sprang to her mind. It was obvious that this was not the time for explanations.

"Hungry?" she asked, simply. "Breakfast won't be long."

"I'll be down when I've had a bath and a shave. Everything all right?"

"Everything," she answered, adding to herself a qualifying "here."

Julian entered the dining room to find nobody before him. He sat down and ate hungrily but hurriedly, and had just finished the meal when Mr. Hurst came in and greeted his son with a lack of surprise that was the result of years of watching his children come and go in apparently aimless fashion.

"Ah, Julian," he said. "Back again."

"Hello, Father." Julian finished the last few mouthfuls and rose. He had no time to waste; he had no wish to become involved in a long and detailed report of his visit to his father's client; he was going to see Alexandra, and at once.

Mr. Hurst seemed to have no wish to know anything about Mr. Randall; he was at the sideboard, lifting the cover off a dish and looking at its contents without enthusiasm.

"Haddock," he mused, helping himself sparingly. "Have the letters come yet?"

"I don't think so," replied Julian. "If they're in the hall as I go out, I'll bring them in."

"Thank you." Mr. Hurst peered over his spectacles at his son's suit. "Isn't that the tweed your mother chose?"

87

"Yes, Father."

"It's made up rather well, don't you think?"

"Yes, Father."

"And it looks warm, too. Decent quality."

"Yes, it is. I'll be off now, Father, I'm in rather a hurry. I'll talk to you tonight about that Randall business."

"There's no hurry," said Mr. Hurst, sitting down and opening his *Times*.

"Tonight," said Julian, from the door.

"After all," came from behind the newspaper as Julian opened the door, "he had a long life, longer than most of us can look forward to with any certainty. Over eighty, if my memory isn't at fault, and very little good done to anybody in all that time, God rest his soul."

Julian had gone out quietly and closed the door; when his father embarked upon a theme, there was no way of telling how long he would be in developing it. The last four words reached his ears, but he had taken three steps along the corridor before their significance halted him. He went back to the dining room, opened the door and stepped back into the room once more, his eyes resting on his father in puzzled enquiry.

"What did you say?" he asked.

Mr. Hurst glanced up from the paper.

"I thought I heard you go out," he said.

"I did go out. I came back again."

"Ah yes, the letters."

"No, not the letters, Father. It was what you said just now about Mr. Randall."

Mr. Hurst frowned; his eyes had lighted on the title of the leading article and he was anxious to find out what they had to say on the subject.

"I said there was no hurry," he said absently.

"But you said— I'm sure I heard you say something about God rest his soul."

Mr. Hurst's frown deepened and his moustache seemed to stiffen.

"I did not speak lightly," he said frostily. "That is a prayer; I meant it as such. When I said that he had done little good in the world, I spoke in no spirit of censure. I—"

"You mean he's *dead?*"

Mr. Hurst laid down the paper, took off his glasses and looked up at his son with his spaniel's look of patient suffering.

"Would I," he enquired, "ask the Almighty for the repose of a man's soul if the soul were not departed? Just tell me—"

"No, Father. I mean, yes, Father. When did he die?"

"I cannot tell you with exactness. The telegram reached the office on—let me see, it would be the twenty-eighth of February."

"But—"

"It stated that he had died peacefully in his sleep the night before; that would seem to mean that he died on the twenty-seventh, but it might quite well be that he died in the early hours of the morning of the twenty-eighth. You must have been the last visitor to that house."

The twenty-seventh . . . Mr. Randall had died on the night he had left for Scotland. The twenty-seventh of February . . . and now it was the eleventh of March. Eleven days . . .

"When will the will be read?" he asked. "Are you sending somebody up?"

Mr. Hurst looked up from his haddock.

"You seem to know very little of what goes on in the firm," he commented. "We cannot spare our men for an unlimited

89

time. Since Mr. Randall had no near relatives, it fell to us to see to the funeral and make the arrangements for the sale of the house and furniture. We did so, but we did so without delay. Your brother went up to Holside himself. Mr. Randall was cremated on the morning of the third, at his own wish—that is, the cremation was his own wish. The date, naturally, had to be arranged by Oliver."

"But . . . reading the will, and so on? I mean, who's up there now?"

"Nobody is up there now," said Mr. Hurst. "The will was read on the same day, and a sad business it was. Only one person present who showed the smallest sign of grief, and that person a man who had been in Mr. Randall's employ for more than forty years. Forty years! There was nothing left to him. Not one penny. The will was made shortly after Mr. Randall's marriage and left his wife his sole heiress; he never changed it except to add a codicil a month or two later to the effect that if she predeceased him, everything he died possessed of was to go to a society interested solely in the collection of old coins. It seems incredible to me that— However, we must not judge. Oliver, I'm glad to say, dealt generously with the old butler, though after forty years' service, it was little enough. He paid his wages for three months and gave him a small bonus and his expenses to his home. There was an old cook, but as she had only served him for a mere twenty years"—Mr. Hurst's precise voice took on an unwonted tinge of sarcasm—"it is not to be expected that he would remember her in his will."

There was silence. Mr. Hurst waited for a comment on his speech, but none was forthcoming; Julian merely stood staring at him.

"I wonder whether you'd mind closing the door, Julian,"

he said at last. "You're causing a draught. If you would come right in, or go out, it would—"

"I'm sorry. I'm going," said Julian. "There's just one thing—would Oliver have the old butler's address?"

"I dare say," said Mr. Hurst.

Julian went out and closed the door behind him. The question of Mr. Randall's four pictures, he decided, could wait; to bring the matter up now would delay him further and lead to long and complicated explanations involving his meeting with Alexandra. The important thing was to see her now—at once. He wanted to ask her a thousand questions, among them what had happened at Holside after he left, how Mr. Randall had died, when she had left the house, whether she knew what was to become of Biscoe? But it would all wait until he had held her in his arms and kissed away the memory of the past few days.

His way lay in the direction of the shop; he would look in, report his return and then drive straight to Nunn Road. Nunn Road, Pimlico—there was nothing romantic-sounding about that; nobody would guess that it was a magic address, that there he would find his love, that there, waiting for him, was Alexandra.

Alexandra. She filled his mind as he drove. He saw her image in every car, in every bus or taxi. She was the slender form disappearing into this shop or the figure vanishing round that corner. He had an exciting sense of nearness to her; only a few streets separated them. Nunn Road; Alexandra Bell; Alexandra Hurst. Mrs. Julian Hurst.

He stopped at the shop, went inside and greeted his aunt, who was showing Mervyn the difference between dusting dust and removing dust. She looked at Julian, as his father had done, without surprise.

91

"Nice to see you back," she said, "but you cut your visit a bit short, didn't you? Did you have fun at Blairwhinnie?"

"No," said Julian. His sense of excitement was mounting. He wanted to talk about Alexandra, but he had resolved that nobody should hear his news until he led her proudly to his mother. After that there would be plenty of time for explanations, exclamations and congratulations. "No, not much," he went on. "And I'm not staying for more than a minute, I just looked in to say I was back. I'll be on the job tomorrow, but just at the moment I've got something important to see to."

"Well, the shop is the thing you're paid to see to," pointed out his aunt. "There must be a girl somewhere, you've got a home-the-hunter, or was it the sailor, look about you. Is she nice?"

"She's adorable. Don't keep me."

"I won't. There's nothing of interest, anyway. It's been quiet here since you left; steady business, but not spectacular. There's only one thing to look at, but it'll keep until tomorrow. I won't sell it until you've given me your opinion on it."

"All right," said Julian, on his way out. "What is it?"

"It's a Clauval, a good one. It was brought in yesterday and I couldn't resist it."

"You bought it?"

"I did. You'll be pleased with it."

"How much did you give for it?"

"I offered two hundred, but she pushed me up to two hundred and ten."

"She . . ." Julian turned and walked slowly back into the shop. "Who brought it in?"

"A girl. It's a pity you weren't here, you would have—"

"Can I see it?" broke in Julian.

92

"The picture? Of course, if you've time. Mervyn, go and get it, will you—and be careful with it. It's the head of a young girl, Julian, but what you'd have been more interested in—"

Julian was not listening. He was bracing himself, squaring his shoulders with a feeling that a weight was about to descend on them. He was fighting a stifling sense of emptiness and desolation. He saw Mervyn approaching with a picture held between his hands; it needed only one glance for him to identify it.

It was the *Green Girl*.

His aunt was talking.

"She wouldn't give her name, but she gave me her address, and I wrote it down. Here it is. Julian, you ought to go and look her up on the pretext of asking her about the picture; she's lovely. But I won't tell you about her now, if you're in a hurry."

Julian went out, but the feeling of urgency had left him. He could not have told why he was so certain that haste would be useless, but the certainty was there and he could not shake it off. His mind was a blank, but he sensed that the journey to Nunn Road would be a wasted one.

Thirteen Nunn Road. . . . He would go and see, of course, because he had to know beyond any possibility of doubt. But he knew already. There would be no Number 13, and there would be no Nunn Road.

There wasn't.

Chapter 6

"No, NOT A middle-aged one," said Julian desperately, at the eighteenth employment agency he had visited in the course of five days. "A—a young one, please."

"Most of our better cooks," said the sour secretary, looking at him over her glasses, "are middle-aged and even elderly. You are thinking, I suppose, as a lot of people do, that the young ones will have a new sort of method, but I can assure you that food hasn't changed, and neither have methods of cooking it." She turned over the pages of an enormous file with as much reverence as if it had been a family Bible. "I have one here," she said, "who might do. She is only thirty-three, and—"

"Oh, no. Twenty-three," said Julian, perspiration breaking out upon his brow.

He felt the secretary's keen little eyes upon him, and knew that she was thinking exactly what the other seventeen secretaries had thought.

"May I have your name and address and telephone number?" she asked, a lurid-looking fountain pen at the ready. "I can then get in touch with you if—"

"No,—oh no! Thank you," said Julian, backing to the door. "It's very kind of you, but I think I'll leave it for the present and do with my—my old one."

He was outside. It was no use. He might go on doing this through the length and breadth of London, and it would do no good. She had gone; she had melted into London's millions. She had gone and he would never find her again—unless she wanted to be found.

In his moments of blackest despair, it seemed to him that she was gone for ever. He had hurt her, abandoned her at the very beginning of their discovery of love, and she had hidden herself away for ever. At other times, when misery lifted for a moment to admit other feelings, he felt the angry bewilderment of a man who has put down something for a moment and, turning to pick it up, finds it gone.

He found, as he had found when he had looked at the picture of the *Green Girl* in the shop and known at once that he had lost Alexandra, that his reason was functioning with less helpfulness than his instinct. His reason told him that a girl had stolen four pictures from him—from the late Mr. Randall—and was now going round London selling them and making a very good thing out of the sales. His reason told him that Alexandra was poor and needed the money; reason also told him that he ought to put the whole matter before his brother who, as Mr. Randall's executor, had a right to know that a certain portion of the estate had vanished. Reason. . . . But reason had given place to instinct, and instinct told him that Alexandra was acting with a purpose. On the surface, Julian knew, the obvious purpose would be to punish him for having left her, but he did not think that Alexandra was a girl who would punish; she would tease, she would taunt, but he was convinced that she would not do anything out of a simple desire to pay him back in his own coin. He deserved it, but Alexandra had no spite in her. She might be laughing at him, but it would be tender laughter; she might be angry, but she would relent and forgive.

It was impossible, he realized, to take his story to his family. His own knowledge that Alexandra was incapable of stealing could scarcely be conveyed to them, and would in any event be contradicted by the facts; she had taken the pictures, given a false address and had sold at least one Clauval. Looked at in the light of reason, the facts were black indeed. His protests would be useless; they would assume that he had been bemused, bewitched. They might even mention the police. The police . . . and Alexandra. It was fantastic—but it was not outside the bounds of possibility.

At the end of a fortnight, he abandoned his enquiries at employment agencies and took to staring into the windows of art dealers' shops. Some day, he felt, there would appear a picture of the head of a girl—a *Blue Girl*, a *Gold* or a *Silver Girl*, and he might then trace the seller and so find his way back to Alexandra. For the moment he had little hope; there was no clue, nothing by which he could trace her. Even the hope of finding her through Biscoe had been quenched; Oliver had paid the old man and then given him his card and told him to come and see him at any time if he needed help or advice. With Biscoe went the last hope of finding out where Alexandra lived; Julian was left to grope—and to hope.

Julian's family noted his preoccupation with varying degrees of concern, but nobody asked a direct question as to its cause. The Hursts, as a family, had an unusual quality of detachment; they went their several ways and seldom expressed opinions on the affairs or the conduct of one another. This was felt by some of their friends to be a commendable form of intelligence and restraint; others were of the opinion that they were all too selfish to bother about anybody but themselves. Whatever the correct reason for their delicacy, Julian was grateful for it. He had reported to his father the fact that he had found two Clauvals—two indifferent Clauvals—in Mr. Randall's collection of pictures, but he had made no mention of the four good ones which he had been entrusted to carry to London. They were not on the list which he had drawn up, and he knew that nobody would know of their disappearance. The pictures, and Alexandra, and all she meant to him—these were matters which he preferred to keep to himself, leaving his family to draw what conclusions they would.

Nannie was the only one who felt impelled to enquire directly into the reason for his moodiness, and was only prevented by Mrs. Hurst's pleading.

"Don't say anything, please, Nannie," she begged. "It'll all come right soon, I hope."

"He's looking roight bad," declared Nannie, "and he don't eat what he used to. And he don't sleep well like he used to do. What's the use of letting him go about looking loike that when a good dose of something would put him roight?"

"But he—"

"Exercoise, that's what he needs," said Nannie. "Shut up in that shop all day long—what he wants is a good long run to shake him up."

"He's worried, that's all, Nannie."

"No, that's not all," declared Nannie. "I've seen him worried lots o' toimes, but never have I seen him on the prowl

97

loike he is now. Up and down the bedroom at noight—I hear him and I'm sure you do, too. There's loikely a girl in the business."

"Perhaps," was all Mrs. Hurst said.

Mr. Hurst, alone of them all, saw nothing unusual in his younger son's demeanour. Oliver, Julian, Drusilla—they had been to him, all their lives, in the nature of Chinese puzzles. He had never understood their characters; he found their behaviour unaccountable and there were times when their very conversation was unintelligible. He came of a long line of quiet, dull but predictable men and women; his children, he knew, were his wife's children far more than they were his; she might understand them, but he could not.

Mrs. Hurst watched Julian with concern and not a little pity; the shadow—whatever was causing it—was deeper than any which had passed over his bright life. Sometimes she wondered whether he had proposed to a girl up in Scotland while on his recent visit to his godmother, and been refused, but he would not, she thought, have taken a girl's refusal in this sombre, passive way. He was a man to ask and ask again, and he knew his powers of persuasion almost as well as she knew them herself. Something had caught him unawares; she could not guess what it was, but she found her maternal instincts giving way before a desire to see how he bore this, his first real experience of adversity.

Drusilla took her speculation to her sister-in-law.

"It's a girl, Madeleine, of course," she said. "Perhaps she's married already."

"Perhaps she's waiting for a divorce," suggested Madeleine, in her cool, sensible way. "Or perhaps her husband won't divorce her—though if somebody wanted to divorce me, I'd let them go at once, wouldn't you?"

"As long as I had enough to live on, I would," agreed Drusilla, with Hurst caution. "But if it meant turning out and earning a living and supporting myself, to say nothing of the children, then I might think twice. Only somehow, I can't see Julian running after a married woman. He's always said that he prefers husbands to wives, and that he didn't see the point of wrecking homes. No, I think what's happened is that he's gone and done it, and some poor wretched girl is going to have a baby. Look at the way he can't bear to look at me. It's a sort of psychological what-you-may-call-it. It brings it home to him."

"But if he doesn't run after married women, she must be single; if she's single, he'd marry her."

"Well, yes—there is that," admitted Drusilla. "It's puzzling, on the whole, because though I think myself that he can be an unmitigated pig at times, he is—to a girl who doesn't see that side of him—quite a catch, in a way."

"He's sweet, but he *is* a bit conceited, you know. No, not conceited, just—"

"Cocksure."

"Yes. It wouldn't really do him any harm to come up against a girl who didn't let him have it all his own way."

"No, but I'd like it to come all right for him in the end," said Drusilla.

"Oliver says we needn't worry about that," said his wife. "He says that he doesn't know what Julian's after, but he's sure he'll get it in the end."

This was perhaps a fair summing up of the general opinion. The days went by and became weeks, and Julian's preoccupation was taken for granted by everybody except his aunt, who began to show signs of restiveness.

"I don't want to disturb you," she said finally, "but I think

I ought to remind you that you're the buyer for this firm. If you'll take a look round, you'll see that our stock's getting a bit low."

"I haven't been back long," said Julian.

"In my opinion," said his aunt, "you haven't got back yet—but we won't go into that. All I want is a nice balance of supply and demand. At the moment the demand is satisfying enough, but the supply is meagre. What's more, you've gone over to the wrong side of the business and bought a picture out of stock. We could have made a nice profit on that Clauval that you've now got hanging in your room. Will you come out of your retreat and attend to business?"

"Yes," said Julian. "I'm sorry."

"That's all right." Her voice softened. "Nothing I can do, I suppose? I mean, if a middle-aged aunt can help a moping-mum nephew, then—"

"No, thanks."

"I didn't think there would be. Well, let me know if I can be of any use."

With an effort Julian forced himself back to something like a normal degree of interest in the shop. There was nothing he could do but wait . . . and wait.

The end of March saw a sharp increase in the tension regarding Drusilla. There were alarms, there were even excursions, and twice Julian was awakened in the middle of bitterly cold nights and instructed to drive his sister to the nursing home, only to be instructed by the sister-in-charge to drive her home again. He behaved with a commendable degree of patience and helpfulness; his embarrassment had long since passed into sympathy, and from sympathy into a sharp anxiety regarding her state—even her fate, for she could not, he was convinced, produce what was obviously an elephantine infant without appalling risk. He helped her in and out of the car with open tenderness and wondered whether, in the worst event, he would be asked to break the news to Cuffy. The monstrous cruelty of a service which kept husbands away from their wives at a time like this had never struck him before; somebody, he felt strongly, ought to do something about it.

The third expedition to the nursing home was not unfruitful; Julian left his mother and sister there at eleven o'clock one moonlit night, and was awakened the next morning by something tugging at his hair. He opened his eyes to find his sister-in-law, in outdoor clothes, sitting on the bed and looking at him with a jubilant expression.

"Wake up, Uncle Julian," she said, prodding him painfully on the chest.

Julian sat up in bed and stared at her.

"What's the time?" he asked.

"Half-past eight on a lovely, sunny morning—and it's all over."

"Over? You mean Drusilla—?"

"Son. The absolute image of Cuffy, only of course your mother thinks he looks a bit like you, too. I was there first thing this morning and they let me in to see him. He's the sweetest thing! And *huge!* Guess what he weighed."

"From the look of it, I should—"

"Eight pounds nine ounces, wasn't it wonderful of Drusilla? The nurses said she was a model; everything went like clockwork. Come on, get up, lazy. Aren't you going to see her?"

"All in good time, all in good time," said Julian, whose relief took the form of irritation. "I can't get up until you get off my bed, anyway."

"I'm going to send a cable to Cuffy," said Madeleine. "You

know, I can't believe the baby's really here. It doesn't seem just over twelve hours since Drusilla was showing me her new picture and wondering what you'd think of it. What *did* you think of it, incidentally?"

"She didn't show me any picture. Get off my bed, will you?" asked Julian. "Time I got up."

Madeleine rose and pulled on her gloves.

"I suppose that by the time you got home from work, she wasn't feeling like showing anybody any pictures, but the man said that there was no doubt that this was a genuine Clauval."

Julian was in the act of retrieving his slippers from under his bed, and wondering how they managed to get themselves there of their own accord night after night. He raised his head and looked up at his sister-in-law with a slowly-awaking interest in what she was saying.

"Clauval?" he said.

"Yes. The old man assured Drusilla that it was genuine, and he—"

"*What* old man?" demanded Julian.

"Why, the old man who brought the picture here."

"The— An old man brought a picture—a Clauval—*here?*" Julian's voice was incredulous.

"Yes."

"To this *house?*"

"Yes. Yesterday, before you came home from the shop. Drusilla was going to ask you about it when you got home, but by the time you got in, I suppose she had other things to think about."

"But"—He was staring at her in bewilderment—"if somebody brought a picture here, and claimed it was a Clauval, where does Drusilla come in?"

"Julian, you don't seem to know what goes on in this house, these days. Oliver and your father have been asking you to join them and give Drusilla something—some sort of present —to celebrate the baby's arrival. It wasn't the arrival, exactly; the idea was simply to take her mind off the imminence of the arrival! You didn't seem to be interested, and so they talked it over in the office and decided to ask Drusilla what she'd like, and Drusilla chose a picture, to keep until she and Cuffy got a house of their own. So your father said he'd ask you to look one out for her, only your aunt said that she'd better do the looking out, as you were—well, she said—"

"Skip what she said."

"I'd be glad to. Well then, this old man turned up un-heralded yesterday. Nannie answered the door and he said he understood that the young lady wanted to buy a picture, and would she care to look at the one he'd brought along which, he said, was a genuine Clauval."

"And you believed him!"

"He said that you yourself had seen it and could guarantee that it was genuine. What's the matter?"

Julian was staring at her with an expression that made her vaguely uneasy; he seemed to be looking through her. She was about to ask him whether he felt quite well, when he spoke in an unfamiliar voice.

"This old man—I suppose he didn't give you his name?"

"Oh yes, he did. Drusilla's not an idiot; she had to give him a cheque because he wouldn't let the picture go until she did, but she made certain she knew who he was and where he came from, so that you could check up."

"I see." Julian spoke slowly and deliberately. "All right; what's his name and where does he come from?"

"His name's Biscoe—oh, you needn't look like that. I saw

him myself—I was here—and he's as honest as the day. You can *tell*. But if you feel doubtful, don't say anything when you see Drusilla, and I'll ask Oliver about it; I didn't have time last night, with all the excitement over the baby."

"I want that address," said Julian.

"Address?"

"The old man, Biscoe."

"I haven't got it—Drusilla knows it; she wrote it down. Julian, I do wish you'd wait until I was out of the room before you—Julian!"

Julian was no longer in the room. One of his slippers was still under the bed; his pajamas lay on the floor; the cord of his dressing gown had caught in the door in his flight towards the bathroom, and was hanging there. The bathroom door had slammed and there was the sound of bath water gushing out of the taps.

Julian was at the nursing home, bathed but breakfastless, within three quarters of an hour. The nurse who answered his summons was kind but firm.

"No visitors," she informed him. "I'm sorry."

"I must see Drusilla . . . my . . . Lady Cuffy. I—you really must let me see her.

The nurse looked at his pale countenance and saw that it was ravaged by anxiety. The memory of all the circumstances came to her in a flash and a sudden, beaming smile illuminated her homely face. She flung the door open wide.

"Why, this is wonderful!" she cried delightedly. "We all understood that you couldn't be here! How well-timed after all, isn't it? I had no *idea* you were coming! Did you have a good journey? But no! We mustn't waste your time—come along, come along."

She hurried him down a corridor and threw open a door; ushering Julian in.

"I won't come in with you," she said, in a low, confidential tone. "You'll want her to yourself, I know."

Julian, bewildered but on the whole uninterested, was already on his way across the room. His sister, to his astonishment, was not lying languidly in bed, as he had pictured her. She was sitting up, leaning against the pillows and looking extraordinarily healthy. She greeted her brother with a cry of astonishment.

"Julian! How lovely of you to come so soon!" She waved an arm gaily and Julian, following its direction, found himself looking at a tiny cot; inside it, he saw a vague little bundle and something that looked like a downy head.

"Yes, yes," he said, throwing into his voice all the congratulation he could muster. "That's fine, fine. Drusilla, I want to ask you something—"

"Say how do you do to your nephew first. Mummy says he looks a bit like you, but that's rubbish—he's the image of Cuffy."

"Good, good," murmured Julian absently. "Drusilla, I—"

"Go on, *look* at him," urged Drusilla proudly. "I know you were afraid he was going to be a baby elephant, but he isn't. Look at him and see."

Julian edged closer to the cot and, groping, found the down and bestowed a few gentle pats upon it.

"Amazing," he said abstractedly. "Drusilla, I've got to ask you something. It's important. You know the old man who brought the picture to the house? Well, I—"

"Picture?" came from Drusilla in amazement.

"Yes, the Clauval. I didn't stop to look at it, but I know— That old man, I must have his address."

His sister looked at him with an expression from which joy and pride were departing, to make room for doubt and suspicion.

"Address!" she echoed incredulously.

"Yes. Madeleine said you had it."

"Well, I have. It was Nunn Road—thirteen, or something. You mean"—To his horror, her eyes filled with tears—"you mean you didn't come to see the baby at all!"

The sentence gathered speed and volume as it was uttered; the last words were a wail of mingled disappointment and fury that brought hurrying footsteps and the anxious face of the nurse round the door.

"Dear me, dear me!" She entered and took charge of the situation with determined calm. "Now, don't worry," she told Julian with a reassuring smile. "Reaction, nothing more; the pleasure of seeing you was—"

"Take him away," wept Drusilla.

"I'm sorry, Drusilla," said Julian, "honestly I am. Look, don't make that row. I'll look at the baby, honestly I will. Look, Drusilla, do shut up, please—*please*. I'll do anything, anything—"

"You can go away," said Drusilla, glaring at him with hatred. "You can go away and stay away."

"I'm sorry, Drusilla. I only—"

"Now, my dear"—The nurse's voice was kind and calm—"you must rest. Just say good-bye nicely to your husband and remember that for the baby's sake you—"

"He isn't my husband," howled Drusilla, the name bringing to mind a flood of memories and a wave of longing. "He isn't my husband!"

"Isn't—!" The nurse's professional manner fell away and horror took its place. "Not your—" She swung round upon

Julian with a face white with outrage. "How dare you!" she hissed. "How *dare* you! To force your way in here and—"

Words failing, she walked to the door and flung it open. The baby, waking up, raised his voice in an angry bellow that spoke so clearly of injury at being left unnoticed that Julian, recalling the horrid scene later, felt that a mistake had been made and that it must, after all, be a girl.

"Outside!" said the nurse. "At once, *if* you please!"

He found himself outside the door marching, or being marched, down the corridor. The nurse, her lips drawn tightly together, opened the front door to its fullest extent, in the manner of one letting in purifying air.

"I needn't tell you," she told him, "that I consider your conduct nothing short of disgusting."

"I had to see her, you see," said Julian desperately. "I—"

"Men!" spat the nurse.

A dim sense of her meaning penetrated Julian's confusion, and he began a protest.

"I'm her brother," he said. "Don't—"

"Don't you try to impose upon me any more," snapped the nurse furiously. "First her husband and now her brother. If you attempt to come here again, I shall inform Lady Cuffy's parents."

The door closed. The outcast walked away, his head spinning. All that—and for nothing. He was exactly where he had been before—at number 13 Nunn Road.

Chapter 7

IN JULIAN'S ROOM there were now two pictures: the *Green Girl* and the *Blue Girl*. He looked at them and felt that they represented two steps in his journey towards Alexandra, and the feeling strengthened his hopes; he was nearer to her; all he needed was patience.

He was less moody, but he was no more resigned; sometimes he had a feeling that she was lost for ever. In his optimistic moods, he felt that somewhere, soon, she would leave a clue; in his worst moment, he felt that she had already left one, perhaps more than one, and he had failed to find it.

His memories of her, he found, were sharpening as the days of separation lengthened. Her image was far away, but it was clear and unblurred; he recalled every trick of movement, every shade of expression. He could hear her voice clearly; again and again he went over the conversations they had had and remembered her blue, lovely, laughing eyes.

Even if he never saw her again, he had, he knew, a remembrance of her that would stay with him all his life. She had laughed at him; she was perhaps laughing at him now, but he was certain that her laughter would be kind, and that one day she would make up to him for the weeks, the months of companionship of which she was depriving them both.

At night when the house was quiet, when the baby's yells for his dinner had been succeeded by the silence of repletion, when Drusilla had had her late bath and banged the bathroom door for the last time, when Mr. Hurst's slow, steady footsteps had gone the round of the house and ended in his bedroom, when sleep descended upon all, Julian found that Alexandra's image became clearest. He remembered things she had said, things they had done. . . .

"Julian, how fast can you run? I used to be good at racing boys twice my size. Ready, steady . . . go."

He had won by lengths, and he had waited for her and had swept her, breathless, into his arms. Alexandra . . .

"Julian, I think I'll make an awfully good wife, but I'm not sure what sort of husband you're going to be. Does your mother spoil you?"

"Good Lord, no! And never did."

"Then what made you so everything-I-want-I-get?"

"If there's no harm in my having it, why not have it? Whatever 'it' is."

"I was thinking of that character you haven't got."

His attention to business was now sufficient to absolve him from the reproaches of his aunt. She knew, as all the family knew in some vague way, that the two Clauvals in his room were the keys to the mystery; Rowena had once or twice, with what she felt to be deep and prepared cunning, remarked on the features of the girl in the picture, but what she learned, that Julian had never seen the original, served only to add to the puzzle. Nor was she helped by a chance remark made by Julian one day at the studio—a remark which caused her to look up from the ledger in which she was writing and fix upon him a look of blank astonishment.

"The Mansion House—yesterday? But yesterday was Sunday!"

"Was it?" said Julian, cursing himself inwardly. "Yes, I suppose it was."

"What on earth were you doing, looking at the Mansion House on a Sunday?" enquired Rowena in a high voice of surprise.

"I suppose," demanded Julian, "you haven't any objection to my looking at the Mansion House if I want to?"

"Well, no. But on a Sunday—"

"You've no objections, I take it, to the way I spend my week ends?"

"Oh, no, no, no. Dear me, no! By no means!" Rowena hastened to assure him. "I merely—that is, if you'll forgive my saying so, it sounded such an *odd* thing to want to do! I mean . . . the Mansion House!"

"If you want to see the Mansion House, then the time to see it is on a Sunday, when the city traffic is off the streets," said Julian. "Is there anything odd about that?"

"Oh, no, no, no! Nothing," said Rowena, "if you *want* to see the Mansion House."

"Well, I did want to. So what?" he enquired belligerently.

"My dear boy," said his aunt, "you can *have* the Mansion House and all its contents, as far as I'm concerned. You can have the Lord Mayor, too. And if that isn't enough, I'll throw in all the Aldermen—will that do?"

"Thank you. If you're looking in on Mother tonight, will you tell her I won't be home? I'm going over to Chelsea."

"You mean to Oliver's?"

"Yes."

"But Oliver and Madeleine are going out tonight."

"That's why I'm going. I'm baby-sitting," said Julian.

Rowena's jaw dropped.

"B-baby-sitting? You!"

Julian made no attempt to clear up her bewilderment. He had lately, in an impulsive moment, offered to take his mother's turn of duty at looking after the young Danny while his parents were out at a dinner party, and he had found that, far from being an occupation which he would take up only under the strongest compulsion, it was one which brought him a peace he found nowhere else. In the quiet house, alone save for his small nephew, he could sort out his thoughts and dream his dreams. Danny accepted from him an abstraction and a detachment which the other members of his family found baffling, and the ritual of bath, supper and bed brought great satisfaction to them both.

"I want that what you're eating," said Danny, perched upon a high chair, pointing to the sandwiches which, as Julian refused to cook or heat food for himself, his sister-in-law left ready for him. "I want those ones."

"You can't have them, said Julian. "My sandwiches are one kind of cheese and yours are another. Yours is the stuff they call, horridly, I admit, predigested."

"Eh?"

"Don't say 'eh,' say 'what.' And don't wipe your hands on your night shirt, use the table cloth. Finished?"

He lifted his nephew out of his chair; a pair of arms stole

round his neck and a soft cheek brushed against his own, giving him an unbearable pang of longing. Alexandra . . .

"Now then"—He tucked his nephew into bed with an expertness that would have astonished his mother—"now sleep."

"Pwayers," said Danny, reproachfully.

"Oh. Well, up you get again, then. Do you kneel on your bed or on the floor?"

"On the wug," said Danny, with a passion for accuracy no doubt inherited from his grandfather. He knelt on the rug, clasped his hands together, squeezed his eyes shut and then opened them again to ask a question. "Shall I say 'Gentle Jesus'?"

"Entirely up to you, old boy."

"Can I sing it?"

"I really don't see why you shouldn't."

Danny shut his eyes once more; there was a pause while he appeared to be selecting a tune, and then he sang the prayer to "Nuts in May."

"Fits pretty well," commented Julian, at the end. "Bit groggy on the last line. Now bed." He tucked his nephew up firmly. "Now straight to sleep."

"No," said Danny decisively. "You haven't told me a stowy."

"So I haven't. Well, what shall it be about? Snow White and the Seven Whoozits, or Hansel and his German girl friend, or Aladdin and the forty juvenile delinquents, or—eh? I mean, what? Well, that seems to me an odd subject to choose, but I'll do my best for you. Cheeses. You ought to have got in a dairy maid; you'd have found her an expert on those matters, and probably on other matters, too, for all you and I know. All right, then, cheeses. Well, there's a sort called Gorgonzola, which doesn't concern you at your tender years, but which has lovely worms running all over it. Then there's the cheese you had at supper, and the cheese I had at supper and the—"

"Not *cheeses!*" shouted Danny, in a sudden access of irritation. "I didn't say *Cheeses*, Uncle Jul-yan. I said *Jesus!*"

Meanwhile, Rowena, sitting in the kitchen at Campden Hill, was reciting to her sister the extraordinary tale of Julian's Sunday pursuits.

"The Mansion House!" she ended. "It's a difficult place to connect with a girl, and yet there's certainly a girl somewhere!"

"Yes," agreed Mrs. Hurst. "I think there is."

"But why the Mansion House?"

"Why St. Paul's? He's been going there every Sunday for the past six weeks."

"*Julian* has?"

"Yes." Mrs. Hurst nodded.

"You mean he's been going to church there?"

"I suppose so; he could go there once or twice or even three times if he wanted to look over it, but—"

"How do you know he goes?"

"Well, Madeleine's got that rather odd uncle who lives at Colchester—you know the one?"

"Never mind about the uncle; get on with the nephew."

"Madeleine's uncle always comes to see them on a Sunday, which is a nuisance, because it means that Oliver has to fetch him from the train and take him back to it again. It chops up his week ends, and he doesn't like it."

"Are we talking Madeleine and her eccentric uncle, or Oliver's week ends, or Julian's love affair?"

"I'm coming to it. You see, Oliver has to drive to Liverpool

Street Station and the old man always makes him go round by St. Paul's so's he can have a look at it."

"I see. And so Oliver's seen Julian?"

"Not Julian, Julian's car," Mrs. Hurst said patiently.

"You can leave your car outside a cathedral without having to go inside."

"You can; perhaps he does. I was only guessing."

"That's what we're all doing—only guessing. Why don't you go to him and ask him straight out what's the matter with him? There's an obvious explanation, of course, but it's a bit early for the cuckoo."

Mrs. Hurst pulled open a drawer of cutlery and stared into it as though she had forgotten her reason for going to it.

"I won't ask straight out," she said slowly, "because that's what you learn not to do after years of dealing with grown-up children. At first, you rush in and try to share their troubles, you let them pour them all out until they've got you as miserable as they are themselves. You spend your days and nights wondering how you can help them, how you can smooth things out, and by the time you've fretted yourself into a fever and arrived at a solution, they've forgotten that trouble and gone on to the next. I used to agonize over Oliver's affairs, and Drusilla's, and Julian's, but I found that that was the way to go to an early grave. What did I want in this drawer, Rowena?"

"Potato peeler?"

"That's it, thanks. Well, as I was saying, I found that my life was being wrecked by my children's passing worries, and so I've learned to keep aloof and to try and give sane, detached advice when they ask for it. I'm sorry for Julian, but I won't get myself involved."

"In my opinion," said his aunt, "this affair of his has gone on long enough. If it was a girl he met up in Scotland, why didn't his godmother write and say so? And where do those Clauvals come in?—because they *do* come in. I thought it might be the girl in the picture, but it wasn't; I thought it might be the girl who brought the picture into the shop— she was a beauty, and just his type—but then it turned out that there was this old man, too. Oliver said that he was butler to Mr. Randall—the old man who died, remember? His idea was that the old butler must have seen how keen Julian was on Clauvals, and had brought one along in the hope of making a good profit on it. But if that was so, why did he offer it to Drusilla, and not to Julian? And why did Julian rush off to the nursing home and make that scene be- fore the baby was half a day old? Do you know, I was there not two hours after he'd been thrown out, and the nurse gave me the most *lurid* account. She finished up by saying that it was a wonder he hadn't turned the milk sour—*disgusting!* Thank God I was never a mother. All that poetry and propa- ganda about the hand that rocks the cradle is all right until you go to a place like that and see all the women laid out in rows and all the babies being carried to and from the ma- ternal founts—*nauseating!* I'm not sorry to have missed it. If I'd thought of it in time, I might have gone to one of those adoption homes and chosen a little boy of about ten, with a dirty face and freckles and his hair falling over his forehead, but no adoption home, of course, would have allowed any child to come anywhere near that revolting man I married, and quite right, too. Is there any sherry? I'd love a drink."

"Help yourself."

"Thanks. I can't stay long; I'm dining out with a fasci- nating man with a pointed beard. I've never dined out with a beard before."

"Why don't you settle down with a nice husband?"

"*Husband?*" The horror in Rowena's voice would have warmed the heart of any feminist. "Husband? My dear, I can't afford one! Look what they cost to feed nowadays! I go home from the shop every evening and spend exactly twenty minutes getting myself a meal of brown bread, butter, an egg and a nicely done salad. Inexpensive and healthy, but a *husband* wouldn't look at it. I'd have to do as you do, live in the kitchen. No, thank you. I'll go on as I am."

"How can you bear those awful parties, clutching a glass and screaming your head off in a stuffy room?"

"They're good for business. How much business do you imagine I'd get if I just sat in the shop and waited for it to walk in?"

"There must be some casual customers."

"About half of them, at a guess. The rest are lured in."

"Well, I still think you'd be better off with a husband."

"No, I wouldn't. Sometimes I do a mental survey of all the husbands I know, and grim it is, too. It seems to me that wives wear pretty well as a rule, but husbands, after the age of about forty, simply fall apart."

"Can't that be the fault of the wives?"

"No; if it were, Edwin would look better than he does. You're a good wife and you've looked after him well—and *look* at him!" Rowena finished her sherry and stood up.

"Are you going?" asked Mrs. Hurst.

"Yes. The smell of those curried beans is making me feel ill. Curried beans!"

"Edwin likes curried beans. Won't you wait and see him?"

"No, I don't think so, thank you. He's your husband and I mustn't speak of him, but my goodness, he *is* a difficult man!"

116

"Difficult? Edwin?"

"Well, I think so. He's difficult to talk to and he's difficult to understand when he does utter some of his sermons, and he's difficult to get anything out of. But I dare say he suits you, darling, and I think you're too good for him. Well, I'd better hurry; he'll be in soon."

In this she was incorrect; her brother-in-law had been home for some time, but a saving instinct had made him pause on his way to the kitchen to see his wife, and sniff the air cautiously. By this means, or by reason of the fact that he heard Rowena's voice, he had ascertained that he would be more comfortable in his study, and here Mrs. Hurst found him some time later, seated in a deep chair, with a drink beside him and an evening paper on his knee.

"Oh, you're here," she said. "I suppose you're hiding from Rowena."

"Has she gone?"

"Yes, some time ago."

"Had she anything of importance to say?"

"No, I don't think so." She hesitated, and then decided to bring up a subject which she felt they ought to discuss. "Rowena thinks that Julian is unhappy."

"Unhappy?" Mr. Hurst emptied his glass thoughtfully and she refilled it and handed it to him. "What makes her think he's unhappy?"

"She wasn't sure. But there *is* something, Edwin."

"Something?" He caught the note of anxiety in her voice and looked up at her over his glasses.

"He's got an odd look, as though he'd lost something."

Mr. Hurst kept his eyes on her while he turned this over in his mind.

"I haven't noticed anything odd about his look. You don't think he's sickening?"

"*Sickening?* Oh, I see what you mean! No, I think he's fit enough, but he isn't *happy*, Edwin."

"Happy," mused Mr. Hurst. "All three of them have always complained very loudly if they weren't, for some reason, happy. They never minded being—"

"I do think we ought to do something."

"They never expressed any desire to be good, or to be useful, but they made a great deal about the necessity for being happy. That is, they always expected somebody else to do something towards keeping them happy. I don't really see that we can go on oiling the wheels, you know."

"They're good children," said their mother, a little doubtfully, "and they're kind and they can be very well-mannered when they like, and—anyway," she ended, running out of assets, "Julian's unhappy."

Mr. Hurst opened his newspaper.

"I imagine," he said judicially, "that the cause is money, or a young woman—or both. He has a great deal too much of both those commodities. Does Rowena complain that he isn't working?"

"No. He's working very hard. But she thinks that his trouble is something to do with those pictures in his room."

"What pictures?"

"One of them came out of the shop; Rowena bought it and Julian bought it from her. The other one was that one of Drusilla's. Don't you remember?"

"I seem to have a vague recollection of something of the kind. But I can't say that I see any sort of connection—"

"Neither do I."

"Well, it will no doubt sort itself out, my dear."

"But don't you think we ought to say something?"

"Say something?"

"To Julian. Shouldn't we ask him what's the matter?"

Mr. Hurst leaned back and prepared to read. He spoke with an air of finality.

"Certainly not, my dear," he said.

"But Edwin, he might want us to help him!"

"That is what I am afraid of," said Mr. Hurst.

Chapter 8

IT WAS A MILD, tender day towards the end of April when the *Silver Girl* appeared. It appeared in the window of Mansard Stevens' shop, which was below the office of Hurst & Son; Oliver saw it on his way to the office and as soon as he got to his desk, picked up the telephone and got through to his brother.

"Julian?"

"Yes?"

"I don't know whether you're interested, but there's another of those pictures downstairs. Down in old Stevens' shop window. I saw it a moment ago and I thought—"

"What picture?" came Julian's voice.

"It's like those two you've got in your room, but it's done in a kind of silver effect, with—" He heard a click and paused. "Are you there?"

There was nobody there. Oliver, with a thoughtful expression, replaced his receiver and sat down at his desk, reluctant for once to summon his secretary and begin the day's work. Facts which he had been turning over in his mind for some time, vague and ill-assorted facts, seemed now to be combining to tell a comprehensible story. Oliver sat gathering them, sorting them, assessing them. That there was a connection between Julian's visit to Yorkshire, his state of mind since his return, and the three Clauvals that had recently come to light, he felt not the slightest doubt. Julian had gone up to Yorkshire on the firm's business; since his return, three pictures, all by the artist Clauval, had appeared in circumstances which pointed clearly to one fact: the seller, or sellers, had chosen to put them in places in which Julian would be bound to see them, or to hear of them. Julian . . . Clauval . . . Mr. Randall . . . the old butler, Biscoe. There was a connecting thread, he felt sure. The girl—for there was, according to Aunt Rowena, a girl, and a pretty one— the girl was difficult to place. There had been no visitors in the house when old Randall died. There had been the butler, and an old cook, but nowhere was there a girl.

It was puzzling; it was rather more than puzzling, for something appeared to be wearing Julian down; he looked and acted like a man . . . Oliver sought for a metaphor, and fixed upon that of a man who paces slowly up and down a platform waiting for a train that has long since left. It was not a good metaphor, but it summed up Julian's air of not knowing quite what he was waiting for.

Oliver, before putting the matter aside and attending to his work, came to a firm decision: he would go up to Campden Hill tonight, and he would see Julian and have a talk with him. The thing had been allowed to go on too long uncommented upon; they would have it out, as they had had other things out in the past, and it might be that he could help his brother in some way. In any event, he would ask him some searching questions and find out what lay behind the mystery. He was glad that he had followed the impulse to ring Julian up; he would know the shop . . .

Julian knew the shop. He also knew Mr. Stevens, and had been at school with his son, who was nick-named Peke for the very good reason that he looked like a somewhat harassed Pekinese. Peke and Julian met frequently, for their friendship had outlasted their schooldays, but they had never met at the office or the shop, for Julian never went to the office, and Peke went to the shop only when the state of his finances made it necessary for him to ask his father's immediate co-operation. Only then did he enter the premises and, on each occasion, emerged after a painful interval, smarting but solvent.

Early this morning, Peke had gone to the shop. A young man upon whom care sat like a feather, and could be brushed off as lightly, he had nothing more upon his mind than the carefully rehearsed sentences with which he intended to refute Mr. Mansard Stevens' inevitable comments upon the ease and speed with which his son spent the money that he himself had amassed by years of hard work.

The words had less effect than Peke had hoped, but at last Mr. Stevens, running out of epithets, had gone upstairs to Mr. Hurst's office, to see if he could get a cheque changed, and Peke stood in the shadows of the shop and brooded with unwonted bitterness upon the harshness of a world in which a parent could talk seriously of letting his only son starve.

His meditations were disturbed by the sound of the shop bell, and after a time—for Peke thought slowly—he became aware that there was nobody but himself to attend to the customer.

He frowned in perplexity. It was very early; though the premises opened before nine, Peke felt that ordinary consideration would prevent clients from intruding before the owners had, so to speak, rubbed the sleep from their eyes. The banks were not yet open; employees were still making their way to their places of employment; Mr. Stevens' own assistant would not arrive before nine-thirty; yet here was a customer, already, waiting confidently for attention. He would have to go forward and do something; he would have to explain firmly that he knew nothing whatever of the business and that Mr. Stevens would return presently.

Peke took a step forward and peered cautiously round a screening picture frame. It would be, perhaps, some eccentric art-lover, long-haired and—

Speculation ceased. Coherent thought ceased. Peke could only gaze, with his mouth opening slowly and remaining open. He was afraid to move, afraid to breathe; he simply stared at the girl who stood in the pale light filtering through the glass door of the shop.

For timeless moments he watched her, and then, as her glance turned this way and that, he felt rather than saw her questioning turn to slight impatience. With a strong effort, he willed his legs to move; they took him unsteadily through a maze of intervening obstacles, and he stood before her at last, his hands squeezed together and his tongue attempting to frame a greeting.

His tongue, unlike his legs, was only too ready to work, but now effort was needed to restrain and not to urge. It was clearly not possible to say those things his tongue was fighting to say. One could not—no, one could not say: *You are beautiful, beautiful; you are the light, you are the morning, for you have irradiated this place, you have transformed it, and you have transformed me, you have turned me, in a moment, from what I was into—into a man. You have shown me a beauty that I never dreamed of; you have . . .*

No, it was not possible. Nor was it possible to say: *This is not my shop; if it were, I would not ask you what you wanted to buy; I would lay the stock-in-trade before you, down there at your lovely little feet. All that I had—if I had it—would be yours, but it belongs to my father, who will return soon from . . . I have forgotten from where, but he will come and thrust me aside and you will turn your eyes away from me and rest them on him and you will be lost to me . . . lost . . . lost . . .*

No, that was impossible too. All speech was impossible. One could only look—and now, as one looked, one saw that she was about to speak. She was . . . yes! She was going to speak to him. To him, Peke Stevens, she was going to speak to him. Her lovely lips were opening . . .

"Good morning," said Alexandra.

Peke's reply was unintelligible, for he was engaged in a process which he would have described as thinking. She thought him a salesman. She had risen thus early, she had sought out this shop, she had entered it in order to make a purchase. Was he now to inform her that she must wait? Was he to confess that he, the man she saw before her, was incapable of attending to her wishes? Was he to put her off, fob her off? Certainly not. If she wished to buy, then he was ready to sell. What was salesmanship, after all, but a projection of one's personality?

"You . . . want something?" he managed to enquire.

"Yes, please." Her voice, he thought, was music, music. "Could I speak to Mr. Stevens?"

"I," said Peke, growing three inches, "am Mr. Stevens."

"Oh. Well, I wanted—"

She paused, and Peke, with growing confidence, brought out his first intelligent sentence.

"Is there any special picture you wanted to see?"

His tone told her clearly that, if there were, it was hers on the spot. She gave him a smile, and when the shop had stopped revolving round Peke, he saw with surprise that she was unwrapping the papers from round something she carried. A picture. She was holding it up for him to see, and the astonished Peke found himself looking at the portrait of a young girl. Over it his eyes met Alexandra's, and he felt himself floating . . . floating—and then without warning, a jarring sound stabbed through his dreams and he came back with a sickening jar to the floor of the shop. Shaken, he stared at the soft, red lips from which the sound had issued.

"You said?" he enquired incredulously.

"Two hundred and ten pounds," repeated Alexandra softly.

"Two . . . t-two . . ."

"I want to sell it. It's a Clauval, you know."

Peke didn't want to know. Moreover, his head effectively cleared, he understood the situation: he had been prepared to hand over to her his father's entire stock of pictures, but she didn't want them. Far from wanting to buy anything, she had come to sell something, and while he had been quite prepared to summon a taxi and load the contents of the shop into it and let her drive away, he was not in a position to meet her request for the fantastic sum of two hundred and ten pounds. Giving away the shop—how easy, how pleasant

125

would that have been—but she didn't want the shop. She had stated her requirements clearly, in five words: she wanted two hundred and ten pounds—and his father, Peke remembered gloomily, was up in Mr. Hurst's office cashing a cheque for twenty pounds, which was all Peke would have in the world until his allowance fell due on the fifteenth of June. The fifteenth of June—and it was now only the end of April. Two hundred and ten pounds . . .

"I'll buy it," he said.

The words came out with terrifying clearness. As Peke uttered them, the door of the shop opened, and Mr. Stevens, senior, stood on the threshold. One glance at his father's face told Peke that his rash promise had been overheard; a stranger could not have read Mr. Stevens' expression, but to his son it said plainly, "Yes, she is beautiful, but business is, after all, business."

"Good morning," he said, closing the door and coming into the shop.

Alexandra smiled at him, and Mr. Stevens, after one keen glance, smiled back. The smile was friendly but brief, and faded as, leaning forward, he took the Clauval from her hands, placed it upon an easel and stood looking at it. Alexandra watched him quietly.

"It's a genuine Clauval," she said at last.

Mr. Stevens nodded, picked up the picture without a word and walked with it into the room at the back of the shop. As he disappeared, Peke relaxed with a sigh. All was well. She was going to get the money; he knew that his father was satisfied. As for himself, here he was in the shop with . . . with . . . Well, yes, that was a point.

"Will you tell me your name?" he asked.

"Alexandra Bell."

"Alexandra Bell," repeated Peke lingeringly. "Alexandra. I like that name. Do you—do you by any chance live in London?"

"Yes, I do," said Alexandra.

"I do, too. I wonder—this is the most frightful cheek, of course, but—well, I do wonder whether we could meet, sometime."

"Sometime, perhaps," said Alexandra gently.

"Could you come and dine and dance then—sometime?" asked Peke, who in moments of excitement had trouble with his sibilants. "Any time you thay—say."

"Sometime," repeated Alexandra. "I'm so glad you bought the picture."

"It was really my father," said Peke, with a burst of honesty. "This is the first time I've ever—I mean, I'm not in the shop, usually, and you're the first — You see, I only came in for a moment to see my father about—about a bit of business, and then he—well, he had to dash upstairs for a few minutes to see a friend of his in an office in the building above—Hursts. 'Matter of fact, the son, Julian Hurst, is an old schoolfriend of mine."

"Really?" said Alexandra.

"Yes. But he's not in Hurst's office. He's in the same business as this, as a matter of fact, he operates in the Kensington district."

"Oh yes?" said Alexandra politely.

"Yes. He's a decent chap, but he"—Peke grinned engagingly—"he's not the fellow you introduce to a girl if you want to keep the girl's attention fixed on yourself—not if you're in your right mind, that is. Not that he's really a risk, if you follow me; he's going to keep off matrimony till he's thirty, he says—and he will, too."

"Oh yes?" said Alexandra, with the same well-bred interest.

"Yes. Sense, in a way, though, speaking for myself, I think that the only way is to wait until you've seen them ... someone"—Peke cleared his throat—"someone you know, at a glance, is—as it were—built to your own specifications. Thomeone you can thee at a glanth is—"

"Yes, I know," said Alexandra. "I think you're right."

"Thomeone," pursued Peke, undaunted, "who theems to have everything you've always—"

"Yes. I know." Alexandra's glance was kind. "What kind of work do you do?"

"Well, I've done this and that," said Peke, after consideration. "You know how some fellows take a bit of time to find their—their—"

"Real bent?"

"That's it. It's all very well for a fellow like Julian, the chap I was telling you about. He more or less fell into it, and he's doing well. But it isn't everybody who—"

"I know." Alexandra glanced, in the kindest way, at her watch.

"You're not—you're not in a hurry?" asked Peke with a sinking heart. "I was going to suggest—"

At this moment Mr. Stevens returned. Instead of the picture, he was holding a cheque book, and Alexandra glanced at it and gave him a mischievous little smile.

"You see, it *was* a genuine Clauval," she said.

"It was. It is," agreed Mr. Stevens, seating himself at a small desk and opening the cheque book. "If I may know your—"

"Alexandra Bell," said Peke. "A-l-e-x-a—"

"Yes, thank you," said his father, unscrewing his fountain pen.

"But look—" Peke's voice had become urgent, and he was fishing distractedly in his pockets. "Look, I don't even know your address!" He produced a small diary and opened it. "Will you—" He looked at Alexandra, hopeful but humble.

"Fourteen Hillmount Gardens," said Alexandra.

Mr. Stevens, seated behind them, raised his head and directed a thoughtful glance at the speaker. He seemed about to say something and then apparently changed his mind. With no more than a lift of his eyebrows, he resumed his writing.

"Four-teen Hill-mount Gar-dens," repeated Peke, writing laboriously. He looked up at Alexandra. "And the phone number?"

"It's in the book," said Alexandra.

"C-could I ring you up?"

Alexandra appeared not to hear him. She had taken the cheque and was putting it into her handbag. She refastened the bag with a decisive little click and then looked at Mr. Stevens. Her voice and manner had a touch of hesitation.

"Will you do something for me, please?" she asked him.

Mr. Stevens gave her a bow that was at once charming, accommodating—and noncommittal.

"Ask me," he invited.

"Will you—could you put that picture into the window?"

"Today?"

"Now," said Alexandra. "I think someone might see it and—"

She paused, and Mr. Stevens smiled.

"It shall go into the window at once," he promised.

"Thank you." Alexandra held out a hand. "Good-bye."

She had shaken hands with him. She had turned and put out a hand to Peke. She was going.

"Oh, but—" Peke clutched her hand desperately. "Look, we *are* going to meet again, aren't we?"

Alexandra released her hand very gently, and smiled at him.

"Yes," she said, and her tone carried comfort and conviction. "Yes, we are."

Julian drove swiftly to the shop, and as he drove, his thoughts sped ahead to the picture in Mr. Stevens' window. It was the third. There was one more. She had sold three of them; perhaps, this time, there would be something to help him, a slender thread that he could hold on to, by which he could reach her. He knew that Mr. Stevens was always in the shop himself; he knew him to be a man of keen brain and keener observation; he would know exactly who had brought in the picture, and he would undoubtedly have asked for details of who the seller was and how he—she—had obtained the picture. It was perhaps too much to hope, but he might . . . he might have got hold of a clue.

Julian parked the car in a side street and went with long, swift strides in the direction of the shop, rehearsing, as he went, the question he would put to Mr. Stevens. He thought once, briefly, of Peke, but Peke, he knew, was never in the shop; his interest in it was purely financial, and his days were too full to allow him to do more than call in occasionally when need drove him.

Julian reached the shop, and his heart gave a bound: there was no picture in the window. A host of fears rushed to his mind; Oliver had been too late. Some . . . someone else had seen the picture and it had been taken out of the window.

Julian opened the shop door, entered and closed it behind him. To his astonishment, it was not Mr. Stevens, but Peke who stood among the pictures, and even through his own troubles, Julian was able to see that his friend was looking a good deal less cheerful than usual. At any other time he would have made some enquiry as to the cause of his dreamy gaze and odd manner, but first things came first.

"Look, Peke," he began without preamble. "I want to see your father."

"I know. It's about that picture, isn't it?" said Peke.

"Yes. Could you—"

"It wasn't the *picture*, Julian old boy." Peke's eyes lit with a reminiscent gleam. "It was . . . Well, I suppose she must have taken me for some kind of fish, standing there and goggling at her, but I—"

"What are you talking about?" demanded Julian.

"The girl."

"*What* girl?"

"The one who brought in that picture. I was standing over there, and I suppose she thought I was—"

"For God's sake, Peke, if you've got to tell a story, then begin at the beginning, will you?"

"That was the beginning!" protested Peke. "That was the beginning! A girl, a beautiful girl, brought that picture in this morning and—"

"Ah!" Julian looked round for a chair, saw none at hand and hunched himself against the beautiful sweep of polished mahogany that served as a counter.

"She was the most beautiful girl I have ever theen—seen," declared Peke. "Ath thoon—as soon as I thor—saw her, Julian, I felt terrible, and I've been feeling terrible ever th—since. I—"

"Wait a minute," said Julian. "Why were you in the shop?"

"I came in for some money," explained Peke simply.

"What time was this?"

"It was early, it was before the banks opened, and that was why my father had to go upstairs and see if he could get me some money. I was waiting for him, and I heard a customer come in and as I was the only one in the shop, I thought I'd better do something. So I took a look before coming forward, and—and then I couldn't say a word. I couldn't breathe. I couldn't—"

"Later," said Julian. "What did she say?"

"She didn't say much. She showed me a picture, and I got the idea that she was selling and not buying, and—"

"Did you know it was a Clauval?"

"I didn't even know it was a picture. I just saw a blur near where she was standing, and then I made out that—"

"And she offered you the picture?"

"I don't know. She smiled at me, and then the next thing I heard was the price."

"The—?"

"She said two hundred and ten pounds."

There was a long pause.

"Two . . . hundred . . . and ten . . . pounds?" said Julian.

"That's what she said."

"And you—"

"I would have given her two thousand and ten."

"So you said it was a deal?"

"Well, at this point, my father turned up."

"What did he say?"

"Nothing, for a few minutes. He looked at the picture and I looked at Alexandra and—"

"She told you her name?"

"Of course. I thought that if my father didn't like the picture, I could find someone to lend me the purchase price, but Alexandra said it was what you said it was just now, a Clauval, and my father nodded his head, and without any more argument he sat down to write a cheque. Just like that."

"And then—?"

"That was all," mourned Peke. "She went."

"She went? But you must have found out something about her? You're not going to tell me that you just stood there—well, perhaps you did, but your father must have asked her where she—"

"Listen." Peke, struck by a sudden thought, was staring at his friend keenly. "Have you seen this picture before?"

"Yes," said Julian. "I have."

"And have you—have you seen her, too?"

"Yes."

"You *know* her?" Peke's voice was high with surprise.

"Yes."

"Then—"

"But I don't know where she is. What I came for was to try and find out what you knew about her. I don't suppose you did more than stand and gape, but if I know your father, he took down some particulars before he parted with over two hundred pounds."

"He knew the picture was a genuine that-thing. And she told me her name and she gave me her address."

A weight that had lain on Julian's heart began to lift.

"Her—" He stopped and cleared his throat. "Her address?" he asked.

"Fourteen Hillmount Gardens," said Peke, and the weight

came down again. "Four—" Peke stopped and his eyes opened wide in bewilderment. "Four— Why—why, that's *your* address, isn't it?"

"Yes," said Julian. "But it isn't hers." He reached out and took his friend's arm in a painful grip. "Look, Peke," he said, "you must have found out more than that! I've got to find her!"

"Why?" asked Peke.

"Because I met her and I fell in love with her and I—I lost track of her, that's why. I've got to find her!"

Peke stood still and stared for a long time at Julian's face, and across his own there passed a succession of emotions easy to read. There was bewilderment and incredulity and, finally, understanding and sympathy.

"What can I do?" he asked at last.

The question showed so obvious a desire to be of use, there was so much comradeship in it, so much sympathy, that Julian was carried back to the days when he and Peke had shared one another's secrets and fought one another's battles. The story, which he had been unable to confide in anybody else, came out in a blessed and relieving torrent, from his arrival at Holside to the time that Alexandra had disappeared, taking the Clauvals with her. He told it all, and found relief in the telling—and something more, for as he spoke, he knew that he was no longer going to wait for clues, for news of Alexandra; he was going out to find her. He told his troubles openly and to the end.

"A cook!" said Peke, his infatuation cured.

"Is there anything wrong with that?" demanded Julian.

"Nothing, nothing," said Peke. "I was only thinking that—"

"Well?"

134

"Don't get me wrong, but it does look as though she got the pictures in a—well, to put it at its kindest—in a somewhat unorthodox way? S-swiped them, as it were."

"I've told you that—"

"But she *took* them," insisted Peke. "She took them, and she's selling them and she hasn't done anything about passing you on any of the proceeds, has she?"

"You've seen her; do you think she could do anything like that?"

"No. Absolutely not. Off her own bat, that is. But sometimes," pursued Peke, his detective instincts roused, "you find that people get behind people and, so to speak, put on pressure. Somebody might be behind her. This Biscoe chap might be—"

"He's nothing but a harmless old man."

"I believe you; I'm only trying to put the other side of it to you. They're in touch with one another, that's clear, and although you know, and I know, that Alexandra's all right, you'd have a pretty poor case if the facts got out."

"I know all about that," said Julian. "And I know something else, too—that I'm damn sick of sitting around waiting for Clauvals to appear wherever and whenever Alexandra wants to plant them. So I'm going to *do* something."

"Do what, though?" mused Peke.

"I'm going to find him."

"*Him?*"

"I'm going to look for Biscoe. If I find him, I find her. I've no clue as to where Alexandra came from, but Biscoe was butler to old Randall for forty years. Nobody, *nobody* would keep a butler for forty years without knowing his address. I'm going back to Holside and I'm going to make enquiries about him up there. Somebody'll know something about a man who was around for all those years."

"Well, you can't lose anything," commented Peke.

"I ought to have done it long ago, instead of hanging round London waiting for Alexandra to spring out of the pavement in front of me. London's too big; I ought to have got back to Holside from the start."

"I see what you mean. Nobody would interest themselves in him or his address here in London, but in those small villages, a fellow need only stay a week end, and when he leaves, they can tell you his history right back to Tudor times."

"There's a fourth Clauval," began Julian. "I—"

"I'll go prowling round the art shops," promised Peke. "I'll be on the lookout. If you'd only had the sense to tell me all this before, I'd have been able to spot Alexandra when she came into the shop this morning. But how did I know who she was? How did I know I ought to have got down on my hands and knees, looking for bus tickets or the kind of soil she had on her shoes, or the bits of the hedge she brushed by on her way here? If I hadn't been bemused, I'd have known at once that the address she gave was yours, but when you catch sight of a girl like that, all unprepared, you—" He broke off. "Here's Father."

There were footsteps in the corridor behind the shop, and Mr. Stevens entered and greeted Julian.

"Your brother rang me up; he says you want the picture," he said. "I've kept it for you."

"Yes. Will you sell?"

"I must make my profit," said Mr. Stevens.

"Nonsense, Father," said Peke. "Julian's an old school friend."

"Quite so," said Mr. Stevens. "But we're not at school now, are we? Two hundred and fifty, shall we say?"

"Twenty," said Julian.

"Fifty," Mr. Stevens smiled. "She was very pretty."

"I'll take it," said Julian. "I suppose you don't—"

"When a lady gives a gentleman's address," said Mr. Stevens gently, "one makes no further enquiry."

"Father, you knew! You let me—"

Mr. Stevens smiled at Julian.

"So susceptible, this boy of mine," he said. "This morning I felt glad—I thought, 'Ah! *he is learning, he has recognized a work of art.'* But then I saw that he was looking at a work of nature. He sent the value of the picture up, of course; she was very quick to see that and take advantage of it. I would like to have her with me in my shop, that young lady."

"Julian wants her in *his* shop," said Peke. "But he doesn't know where she is."

"She is not at Hillmount Gardens?" enquired Mr. Stevens smoothly.

"She never was," said Julian.

"She didn't—" Mr. Stevens' manner became professional— "she didn't get that Clauval from you . . . dishonestly?"

"No," said Julian.

"Father, what a silly idea," said Peke.

"Ah—" Mr. Stevens relaxed. "But there's a lot of that kind of thing done, you know."

"Yes, I know," said Julian. "I'd be awfully grateful if you could tell me if you ever find out her address. We met and I very stupidly let her go without finding out where she lived."

"Sometimes that isn't so stupid," said Mr. Stevens.

"I shall look for her," promised Peke. "I'll start now."

137

"Yes, do that," begged Mr. Stevens. "It will be a great relief to me. You have been in the shop for too long, and you are not much of a help and you are also not much of an ornament, though that, of course, is my fault and not yours. If the young lady comes in again, my dear Julian, I shall detain her, by devious means, until you come round and claim her."

"Thank you," said Julian. "You've very kind."

"Not at all." Mr. Stevens bowed. "Would you care to sit here and write your cheque?"

Chapter 9

JULIAN, having made up his mind to go back to Holside, wasted no time. He had first to inform his aunt that he would be away for a day or two, and he did so without preliminaries, on the evening before his intended departure. Rowena was paying one of her frequent visits to Campden Hill before going on to dine at her own home; she and Mrs. Hurst were enjoying their usual exchange of news, an unfair exchange, since Rowena always had a great deal of outside gossip to impart, while Mrs. Hurst's contributions were of purely domestic interest. They were in the kitchen, and Rowena was watching—with a sense of wonder that the sight always brought her—her sister's evident enjoyment while engaged upon such tasks as mincing beef or putting potatoes through the masher.

"How's Drusilla?" she asked.

"Oh, she's just like her old self, thank goodness, and the

baby's a dream. I was thinking about her a moment ago and wondering how she'd manage on the plane going out to Cuffy."

"I hope she'll find somebody who'll hold the baby while she's being airsick," said Rowena. "I'm thankful it won't be me. Isn't it odd? I must be the most unmaternal woman ever born, but wherever I go, women press their children on to me; will I mind this little one or keep an eye on that little one, and so on. I think I must have a kind look, don't you?"

"Not at all; all you've got is an unoccupied look."

"Oh. Thank you. Did I tell you that Kitty—Kitty Long, you remember her?—is going to have yet another operation?"

"*Another?* She's had two!"

"Yes. She says she enjoyed the last two so much that she's looking forward to the third. I forget what they're slicing off this time, but it's coming off from her inside, but as I told her, there can't be much left to hack off. The woman must be a mere shell. Doctors!" Rowena's scorn filled the large kitchen. "I've told Kitty that every time this doctor of hers wants to take his family off for a holiday, he gets the money by advising all his women patients to have operations. How else do you think surgeons live in the style they do? By chopping up all these rich, idle and half-witted women like Kitty. Every time she eats something that disagrees with her that man hacks out another bit of her inside. And diet! First he got her off decent meals and on to nuts and carrots and shredded horse-food. Then when all that chewing made her teeth wear out, he switched her on to fruit juices and disgusting-looking squashy vegetable mixtures. Then he put her on to bread that's got nothing in it but lumps and toe-

140

nails. All between operations, of course! I've known silly women, but she really— Are you listening?"

"Yes and no," said Mrs. Hurst. "Oliver's coming to dinner with Madeleine tonight. She's a bit worried about Danny."

"What's wrong with Danny? Oh, you mean that business of jazzing up his prayers. Nonsense! I do .wish you'd tell me why everybody sets out to make sure that Heaven's going to be such a damn dull place? When I get there, I'll kneel straight down and sing 'Gentle Jesus' to the tune of 'Girls and Boys, Come out to Play,' and God'll come out and say, 'Well, that's the nicest sound I've heard since they composed all those nice new tunes for those dreary old hymns!' What does Oliver think about it?"

"Well, I don't suppose Oliver would mind if Danny got on his knees and recited verses out of the Koran; he says the main thing is to get them down on their knees."

"Well, that's a broad enough outlook. He— Oh, hello, Drusilla."

The door had opened to admit Drusilla, rosy and tumbled from giving the baby his dinner and settling him into bed.

"Hello, Aunt Rowena. How's business?"

"Not bad. It's nice to have Julian's mind on it again."

"Any new clues about what's eating him," asked Drusilla, going to the refrigerator and pouring herself out a glass of milk.

"None. Three pictures, that's all; I suppose you've seen them in his room?"

"Yes; green, blue, silver. He *looks* better, somehow. But he hasn't taken a girl out, or rung a girl up, since he came back from Scotland. Pity I'm married, in a way; I think that if I'd still been single, he'd have told me. Aunt Rowena, why do you drink sherry in the kitchen? Why not come into the—"

"The kitchen is the only place I can see your mother. If you were going to suggest the study, I can tell you that that's where your poor old father hides when he hears my voice." She gathered her things together and rose. "Well, I must go. I don't have to go up and bend ecstatically over your little treasure in his cot, do I, Drusilla?"

"Certainly not; I won't have him breathed on."

"Good. Well, good-bye. No, don't come out, Dru."

She made her way to the hall, and Julian, letting himself in at the same moment, held the door open for her and then, coming to a sudden decision, closed it again.

"Have you got a moment?" he asked.

"Only one. What is it?"

"It won't take long," said Julian. "I would like to go away for a day or two."

"Oh. When do you want to go?"

Julian's answer was made in a tone which did not encourage comment.

"I'm going tomorrow morning," he said.

His aunt made no reply, but her eyes met his and there was an expression in hers—a mixture of exasperation, bewilderment and sympathy—that made him add an impulsive sentence.

"I know I'm being a bit trying," he said, "but the fact is that I—I've lost something. I'm going to try and find it, that's all."

"All right," said Rowena with unwonted gentleness. "I hope you do find it. I know it's a girl, and I hope she's a nice one."

"She's a cook," said Julian brusquely.

There was a long pause while his aunt took in this piece of information. Then, as she did not speak, he gave her a half-scornful smile.

"If you're feeling nervous," he said, "I can reassure you. She can give Drusilla points—on looks, behaviour and even accent. Any comment?"

"Yes," said Rowena, crisply. "If you mean to tell your mother, don't just throw the information at her in that come-on-and-fight-me manner. You've had your fists doubled up at the ready ever since you came back to London, and you must be tired of waiting to find someone to use them on. We've all taken a great deal from you lately in the way of odd behaviour, and we'll be very much relieved when you come out into the open and give us some idea of what's gnawing at you."

"I said she was a cook, that's all. That's the thing people will fasten on, after all. She *is* a cook."

"All right, she's a cook. Nowadays most girls train as cooks. Barons' daughters learn to be cooks. Peers' daughters probably become cooks in this generation, but your mother and I belong to the one that's gone, or going, and a cook, in our day, wasn't a ravishing creature in high heels and a pale pink overall; she was a formidable woman, middle-aged, who graduated from scullery maid and went out with policemen on her day off. So when you tell your mother, you might use a bit of imagination and try to see it from her point of view. You're a man of twenty-seven, not a boy of seven. If you're in trouble, let somebody with a better head than yours get you out of it. If you've mislaid a girl and she's a nice girl, let's all have a hand in searching for her. God knows we could do with a cook in this family to give your mother a bit of relief from preparing vast meals for you and your

143

poor old father. Tell us who she is and where you found her and where you lost her and why, and stop walking round like a belligerent so-and-so looking for someone to smack on the head with a knuckle duster. Go on to wherever you're going tomorrow to look for her, and if you don't find her, come back and let keener intellects in the family have a go at it. Now open that door and let me get out and get a good walk and some fresh air. Thank you. Good-bye. And"— The last came over her shoulder as she walked away—"good luck to you."

The words cheered Julian as he drove up to Holside very early on the following morning. It was a lovely day and, although he was leaving spring behind as he drove north, the changes in the look of the countryside afforded an interesting and pleasant change from the conditions under which he had last set out to Holside.

When he reached the village, he drove straight to the inn. He switched off the engine of the car and sat in the silence, and Alexandra seemed to open the door and climb in beside him, as she had done so often in the past. He felt a sense of ease and comfort; since his departure from London, he had had a feeling of coming nearer to her, a feeling that the long parting was over, and he was on his way . . . somewhere . . . to meet her.

He looked round the little courtyard of the inn; there was nobody about, but it was past noon and most people, he knew, would be indoors having their midday meal. He went into the little hall, and the well-remembered figure of Mrs. Cole came bustling and rustling down the passage.

"Why, Mr. *Hurst!*" she exclaimed. "Well now, it's nice to see you back in these parts!"

"It's nice to be back, Mrs. Cole. How are you?"

"Ah'm fine, Ah'm fine, and so's business. We're all fine. Have you come to stay in Holside?"

"Well . . . not exactly," said Julian. "As a matter of fact, I'm here"—He brought out the words he had rehearsed on the way up—"I'm here to try and find out something about old Biscoe—you remember the butler up at—"

"Butler to Mr. Randall? Aye, Ah remember him, of course," said Mrs. Cole. "Don't let's stand talking here in this draught, Mr. Hurst; come into the parlour and sit you down and let me bring you a nice bite o' lunch. I've got a bit of boiled beef you won't say no to, Ah'm sure, with some potatoes and a nice dish of vegetables and a bit of cheese to follow—how'd that be?"

"It sounds magnificent."

"Well, sit you down there by the fire, and Ah'll have it ready in no time. Will you drink a glass of beer while you're waiting?"

"I'll try," promised Julian with a smile.

"Oh, ho, ho!" Mrs. Cole's laugh came out in an infectious roar. "Ah'll fetch you some, then, and you can start trying. And then you can tell me what you want and we'll see if we can get it for you."

Julian poked the fire into a blaze, drew a chair close to it and settled down in quiet comfort to await his lunch. The peace of Holside, after the roar of London and the rush of the journey, calmed his spirit and relaxed his limbs. The beer brought an added restfulness, and by the time Mrs. Cole came in to lay the table and set out his meal, he was filled with dreamy contentment.

The food was excellent; Mrs. Cole left him to enjoy it and went away to eat her own, and it was not until the remains of the lunch were cleared away that she drew up a chair opposite to Julian's and allowed him to state his business.

"Now, what's this?" she asked. "You want to know some't about old Biscoe? He's gone, you know; he went soon after old Mr. Randall died."

"I know, but my father's firm is clearing up the estate, and they find that they haven't got an address by which they can trace him. I came up to try and find out if anyone here knew it."

"His address?" Mrs. Cole's large, red hands were outspread upon her knee and her face was intent and frowning in concentration. "You mean you'd like to know where he went off to?"

"Yes, or where he used to live. He came from London, I understand."

"Oh, he was a London man," said Mrs. Cole. "He was that; you wouldn't have thought it to hear him speak, but Mr. Cole—Mr. Cole was alive then—he asked him one day, straight out, and Mr. Biscoe said that was right, he was a Londoner."

"Did Mr. Cole ask him his address?"

"His address in London?" Mrs. Cole, after sitting for a moment in thought, shook her head slowly from side to side. "No. No, I don't think he ever did."

"Would anybody here have known it?"

Mrs. Cole was certain that they wouldn't.

"Nobody," she explained, "ever rightly knew him. He didn't come in here more than three times in all the twenty years they were here. At first Mr. Cole said to me, 'Likely his old master don't like him coming down for a drink,' and he was right. Mr. Randall lived here all those years, but not a penny-worth of business came to anybody in the neighbour-

146

hood, unless it was the grocer and the young lads who used to pull the stores up the hill in winter. What he wanted he got sent up from London; as far as us here was concerned, there wasn't a penny in charity or a word of sympathy when anything went wrong, and not a finger put out to help a living soul. Nobody wants to speak ill of the dead, Mr. Hurst, but Mr. Randall was a mean and a hard old body, and that's the truth. How people could live out all their lives alone like that, with never a pleasant word from a neighbour, or a smile, or a chat, is what Mr. Cole never understood to the day he died. Time and time over, he'd say to me—"

"Would anybody have any idea?" put in Julian as gently as possible before the late Mr. Cole's utterances could be related.

"Not a soul, Mr. Hurst. The only thing you could do, maybe, is to go up and see the general."

"The—?"

"You remember General Whitlock, who used to live next door to Mr. Randall?"

"No, I—"

Julian fell silent. Yes, he remembered. He had never seen the general, but he remembered Alexandra's introduction to their neighbour.

"Julian, have you ever seen a hat walking?"

"A hat? All right, I give up."

"But it's true; it's real; it's a fact. Come and see."

They had gone and he had seen—a hat walking along a hedge. A pork pie hat, green, a somewhat mildewed-looking felt hat moving steadily along the top of the hedge as the man next door, whose head reached exactly to the top of the hedge, walked in his garden. Yes . . . he remembered.

147

"He's not next door any more, you know," said Mrs. Cole. "He moved into The Manor as soon as he could get into it."

"Oh, did he buy it?"

"He did, and pleased we all are. A good long time he waited for it. Go on up and see him, Mr. Hurst. He'll help you, if anybody could. He used to keep two servants, and they used to talk to Mr. Biscoe sometimes and he might have told them something that would help you. Go on up and ask the general."

"I think I will."

Julian thanked his hostess, paid his bill, drove the car up the hill and turned into the drive of the well-remembered house.

The change in it, since his last visit, was startling. Mr. Randall's neglect of the gardens had been succeeded by an order and neatness that had the touch of a loving hand. The house itself was freshly painted; the windows were open and pretty curtains hung within, some of them fluttering in the breeze like flags of welcome. Julian, getting out of his car and looking about him, felt an unexpected and fleeting regret for old Mr. Randall, all sign of whom seemed to have been painstakingly obliterated.

He stood at the front door, as he had done on the dark night in February, and it seemed to him that he could hear Alexandra's light footsteps inside the house. He had stood here and she had known of his coming and she had looked over the banisters to assure herself that he was the type who wouldn't feel the cold, who wouldn't notice how much coal there was or how many blankets there were. Alexandra . . . curled up on the hearth rug, warm and cozy—and he had walked in like a rough, overbearing, arrogant, ignorant fool and . . .

148

He shook himself out of his dreams and made to ring the bell. His hand was on it when he heard the scrunch of footsteps on the gravel, and turned to find himself looking at a tall, thin man with gray hair upon which was a hat which Julian had no difficulty in recognizing.

Julian, have you ever seen a hat walking . . . Julian, have you?

The voice of the hat's owner came to him and roused him.

" 'Afternoon. You looking for me?"

"How do you do? I'm sorry to come along without warning like this," said Julian, "but I was in the village and they told me—"

"Ha!" broke in the old gentleman. "Know you now. Got your face. Knew I'd seen it, but slipped m'memory for a second. Sign I'm getting on. Used to see you here in that old . . . in Randall's time."

"Yes. I was here for—"

"Ha! With that pretty-as-a-picture girl they said was a cook, but I never believed it; not on your life, I said; what would a girl with a complexion like that be doing in front of a stove? What were you doing up here?"

"I was here for a short time, looking over Mr. Randall's collection of pictures."

"You weren't looking over them when I saw you," remarked the general. "Let's go inside out of the wind, and have a drink. My name's Whitlock. General. What's yours?"

Julian told him, and followed his host indoors.

"What're you doing up here?" asked the general, when they were seated in the room into which Biscoe had shown Julian on the night of his arrival, a room which, once so comfortless, was now bright with rugs and pictures and chintz-covered chairs. "Thought of you, once or twice, but not alone like this. I'd got you teamed up with that girl, but perhaps you got there too late, hey? They say men are scarce in this country, but whenever I came across a girl I fancied, sure enough, somebody'd snapped her up before I got there. Come over here and choose your drink. Can't get my wife in to meet you; she's gone off on a shopping jaunt to London. That'll land me in for a nice bit of money."

"How long have you been in this house, sir?" asked Julian. "It's nice to see someone in it who knows how to make it look its best. It used to be—"

"Damn waste," said the general, "but it wasn't my fault. I would have had the place twenty years ago if it hadn't been for that old . . . for old Randall. He did me down. Can't call him names now that he's dead, though 'pon me soul I can never see why not. I would have had this house long ago, but I made the mistake of letting him see that I wanted it, and that was enough; he'd have given his last penny to keep me out."

"Were you a friend—did you know him before he came here?"

"Never set eyes on him in my life, and only saw him twice after he came here—couldn't avoid it, both times, or I'd have done so. The man was a . . . well, he's dead, as I said. But I've lived in these parts all m'life, and my wife and I had our eyes on this house from the first moment we saw it. We both fell in love with it, and we decided that if ever it was put up for sale, we'd buy it. Well, it was; it was put up for auction and I never had a doubt I'd get it. But I was walking round looking at it when that old . . . when old Randall drove up, and I talked too much. I suppose I sounded cocksure, too, and why not? I felt cocksure. I was telling him how I was going to change the garden round, I remember. I suppose he laughed up his sleeve—no, he couldn't laugh. I had three children, all young, and I pictured them growing up in the house. Well, to cut it short, old Randall sent a man up from some infernal firm of lawyers in the city, with orders to go to the limit. I went as far as I could and then I went as far as I dared and then I had to drop out, with my wife standing beside me, looking— Well, we were all a bit upset, I can tell you. After the sale, I went round mortgaging myself up to the eyebrows and then I went to old Randall and I said, 'Look here, you're a man alone and I'm a man with a family; this house needs a growing family.' I offered him a good bit more than he gave for it, and he turned it down flat, and in a way I won't forget. And then what did he do but turn the place into a ruddy warehouse for his furniture and pictures, and let the garden go to the devil."

"Well, you're here now," said Julian consolingly.

"Yes, and the children are here, but they're my grand-children and I shan't see 'em grow up here. I bought the house next door a few years ago, when I'd given up hope of old Randall ever dying. When he did die, I made certain this time that I'd get the place, and cheap—shifty lawyers or no shifty lawyers."

"It's my father's firm."

"Eh?"

"It's my father's firm."

"What—those lawyers?"

"Yes. I only—"

"Well, I did 'em down," said the general proudly. "Right in the eye. When the house came up for auction, what did I do? I got the whole village behind me. Every man jack. Every time a prospective buyer put in an appearance, there was someone in the offing to put in a word about drains or ghosts or pestilence. We started a whispering campaign and by God, it worked! It worked. There wasn't a decent bid at the sale, as you'll know if you take an interest in your father's business. No reserve on it; bad business for the heirs and assigns but good business for me. I got it for a song; if it ever does have a ghost, it'll be the ghost of old Randall standing at the foot of my bed with an auctioneer's hammer, trying to put the fear of the devil into me. Well, that's that; don't know why I told you, but I hope you'll tell your father. I'm a happy man today and m'wife's a happy woman; if you can find a nicer house than this in the whole of England, you're welcome to go and live in it. Another drink?"

"Well . . . thank you."

"What're you doing here?" asked the general, pouring it out.

"I'm on a sort of quest. I'm looking for someone who can tell me where I can find the old butler Mr. Randall had."

"Old Biscoe. Well, had any luck?"

"Not so far."

"He was a London fellow, I understand."

"Yes, but that's all anyone seems to know."

"Nobody ever found out much about old Randall or his affairs. He came here, it's said, when his daughter skipped off with someone and married without his consent. He used to live in the West Country, near Exeter, but nobody knows quite what made him sell up there and come and live in the north. Things used to leak out now and then, servants' gossip, mostly. All I know is that when he came here, he only furnished a few rooms, and then he pushed all his other stuff wherever it would go, and put the lot under dust sheets. All he needed, as I told him on the only occasion I got the chance, was a two-roomed cottage with a warehouse behind it. And whatever it was that happened before he left Devon, I don't think he cared much. That's to say, I don't think it went very deep. He was sour, if you understand me, but not soured. He was a self-contained fellow and I don't fancy he wasted much in the way of emotion all his life. All he was really interested in was that coin collection of his, and a fat lot of good it did him. Chap's dead now, but if one single soul in the world regretted his going, I didn't see any sign of it. Nobody at the funeral except the poor old butler. No sign of that pretty girl. What became of her?"

"She's in London."

"Ah-ha! That came out pat! Well, bring her up here to see us when you've got fixed up together, if you're going to get fixed up together. You going to get fixed up together?"

"Yes. We are . . . eventually."

"Well, take my advice and cut out the eventually. Life's too short to waste any of it without a pretty girl like that beside you. And a cook, to boot. You got to go?"

"I'm afraid so," said Julian, on a note of dejection that brought the older man's eyes to rest on him for a moment in speculation. "I haven't found out what I came to find out."

"Well, you came to the wrong place," said the general in his brisk accents. "You can't find anything if you look in the the wrong places, y'know. Why don't you go back to the source?"

"The source?"

"Yes. Randall didn't belong here, so if you want to know anything about the old servant, I'd advise you to go—if you've time, that is—to his old house down in Devonshire. Old Randall lived there all his life until he took this house. They'd know something about him and his affairs down there. Go down and ask the people who bought his other house."

"I don't know the address."

"Well, I do," said the general, "and so should you, too. You ought to have gone to those lawyer Johnnies and got them to give it to you before you posted off on a wild goose chase. He came from a place called Thorley Grange. If I'm not mistaken, you get to it by way of Honiton. Care to look it up on the map?"

They looked at the map, but Thorley was not marked. The general walked out to the car with Julian.

"Like to know how you get on," he said. "But that's where you should have gone in the first place. Take my word for it, they'll tell you something down there."

"Twenty years is a long time."

"Not down in Devon. You don't get those foot-loose types down there. You get the permanent people; none of those Johnnies who buy a place near London and only use it as a dormitory. Well, good-bye. Let me know how you get on."

"Thanks very much, sir, I will."

"And bring that pretty girl to see me. She used to peep at me through the hedge; I caught her at it. Bring her up and I'll ask her what it was about me that drew her. Good-bye, young fellow. And I'll give you a bit of advice: if you're looking for what I think you're looking for, then stick at it until you find it. Good-bye! Good-bye!"

Julian looked back when he had reached the gate; the old man was still standing at the front door. Raising his hand in a final salute, Julian drove through the gateway and turned the car's nose towards Devonshire.

Chapter 10

JULIAN STAYED that night at an inn of which, on his arrival, he could see little. He awoke next morning to the sound of birds twittering and water gurgling, and got up to find that his window overlooked woodland and water, birches and brook. He bathed and dressed swiftly, to hear, on going downstairs, almost as pleasant a sound as those to which he had wakened: the sound of frying. Bacon, his nose told him.

He sat down to a breakfast of porridge, bacon and eggs, toast and honey-in-the-comb, hot scones and coffee with lumps of Devonshire cream floating on it. Afterwards, he paid his bill with an unusual feeling that he had got, this time, his money's worth; then he got into the car and drove out to find Thorley Grange.

He found Thorley Village without difficulty; it was in a valley, and on the hillside, Julian could see a wood and what he took to be a large building. He felt that this might be his objective and, turning off the main road, began to climb, but the hill road was so narrow and so tortuous that he began to have doubts of its leading anywhere at all. He was relieved to see ahead of him the figure of a short, stout man plodding purposefully uphill, and drew up abreast of him to ask the way.

"Can you direct me to Thorley Grange?"

"I'll do more than direct you," said the man. "I'll take you there. I'm just on my way. It's such a beautiful morning that I thought the walk up and down might do me good, knock a few pounds off." He gave a jovial laugh and, without waiting to be invited, made his way round to the other side and got into the car. "You keep on this road. Are you a father, by any chance?"

Astounded, Julian could only answer that he was unmarried.

"Thought you didn't look old enough," said his passenger. "You'll be a cousin or a brother, of course. My name's Glitter; I'm a doctor. Lot of Glitters hereabouts, and of course a lot of jokes about all that glitters. Look out; I'd go a bit slow just here if I were you; those little beggars pop across the road like rabbits. You can't stop 'em, they will do it, but not many people use this road, and those who do, expect 'em to pop out, and go accordingly, so there's no real danger. There's another lot—look out!"

The warning was a necessary one. Parties of small girls were appearing from the woods that bordered the road, and were tripping across without look or pause to the other side. Julian, slowing down to what appeared to be the regulation walking pace, looked out at the young figures against the picturesque background and felt a strong desire to put the scene down on canvas. The sky was a clear blue, the grass had all the freshness of spring; the leaves were a tender green, the girls were in long, scarlet cloaks with peaked hoods beneath which could be seen bright eyes and glowing cheeks. Everywhere was colour and movement and a look of newness.

"Nice-looking lot," he commented, as he slowed up to allow several groups to cross the road. "About what age would they be?"

"Oh, they're just sprats," said Mr. Glitter. "They range from about nine to about twelve. Healthy lot; I ought to know, because I look after them all."

"Where's the school?" enquired Julian, and saw the doctor turning to stare at him open mouthed.

"School? Good Lord, we're going there!" he exclaimed. "You said Thorley Grange, didn't you?"

"Well . . . yes," faltered Julian. "I did, but I didn't know—"

"It's been a school for nearly twenty years," said the doctor. "You're a bit behind the times, aren't you?"

"I—well, yes. As a matter of fact, I—"

"Well, I've only been here myself for a matter of nine or ten years, but Miss Raikes bought it about twenty years ago and turned it into a girls' school. She's the principal, not the headmistress. I've never quite discovered what their separate functions are, but they don't like you to mix them up. What are you stopping for? Lost your nerve?"

"I'm not exactly keen on walking into a girls' school," admitted Julian.

"Oh, come! They're nothing but little 'uns, after all, and it isn't a very big school, as schools go. I don't suppose there are more than eighty of them, all told."

"Eighty!"

"Ha, ha, ha!" The doctor's laughter rolled out of the car and over the hillside. "Well, well! I never saw a young man turn pale at the thought of getting into a girls' school before. But if you're really frightened, I tell you what we'll do: I'll walk up to the sanatorium, which is in a separate building, and you can leave the car here—draw into that bit there— and I'll show you a way you can walk up to the Grange without driving up in full view. This path'll take you up to Miss Raikes's own room. Will that do?"

"Thank you. Can't you—"

"I can't go with you, if that's what you were going to say. My way lies over there. You go this way. Make for those trees and then cut up the hill and you'll see the house above you."

They got out of the car and the doctor stood watching Julian climb a gate and start up the hill.

"Don't lose your pluck," he called.

Julian grinned at him and went on his way. The wind was blowing keenly, searchingly; the air in his nostrils was pure and bracing. The valley lay at his feet, and the whole new, green prospect seemed to be smiling in encouragement. His spirits rose in thankfulness at the knowledge that at last he was acting. He was moving, he was searching, struggling towards Alexandra instead of merely waiting.

The mood stayed with him and made his opening sentence to the tall, elegant principal firm and business-like.

"I won't keep you," he told her. "I'm here on a rather pointless errand and I'm afraid you'll think that I'm wasting your time. I ought to explain, first, that when I was on my way here, I had no idea that Thorley Grange was a school. If I'd known, I would have telephoned and asked you to see me, but as I was driving up, I met the doctor and he advised me to leave my car and walk up over the hill."

"I shall be glad to help you if I can," said Miss Raikes, in a voice as cool and sensible as her manner. She seated herself and waved a long, white hand. "Won't you sit down?"

"Thank you. I came here," said Julian, "to ask whether you knew anything of a man named Biscoe."

"Biscoe!" The two syllables were long drawn-out and thoughtful. "The only Biscoe I ever heard of was an old man who was butler to a Mr. Randall who used to own this house."

"That's the one," said Julian.

"He must be very old now," said Miss Raikes. "He's not in trouble, I hope?"

"No. That is, not as far as I know. I'm looking for his address."

"His address?"

"Mr. Randall died two months ago and left Biscoe nothing. My father's firm are the executors, and they're anxious to find him with a view to doing something for him, if possible."

"If you feel that Biscoe would have been disappointed at being left nothing," said Miss Raikes, "then I can assure you at once that, knowing Mr. Randall as well as he knew him, he would have expected nothing. Was Mr. Randall ill for long?"

"No. He died very suddenly."

"Was he still in the house at Holside?"

"Yes."

"An odd man," mused Miss Raikes, carried back to the past. "A very odd man and in many ways a hard man, but when people call him a bad man, I always have to disagree. Did you know him well?"

"No. I met him twice."

"You sound as though you had disliked him."

"I can't say I felt drawn to him, exactly."

"Nothing interested him but his collection of coins," said Miss Raikes. "He hadn't very much sense of personal relationships. He lived in himself and for himself."

"Did you know him long?"

"Oh dear me, yes. I knew him all my life. His wife was my greatest friend. You would think that marriage with a man of that kind would have been a miserable sort of affair, but she was a woman with a very happy disposition, and she had a great many interests. Domestic interests, of course; you must remember that I'm speaking of a time when women found plenty to interest them in their homes. I was in this house a great deal before I ever thought of buying it; indeed, I could have been in it permanently, and on the same footing as Mrs. Randall, as she well knew, because—one can speak of these things when they're so long past—Mr. Randall's idea of getting himself a wife was scarcely romantic; he simply proposed in turn to all the young women in the neighbourhood—I was one who had the doubtful honour—and he married the first one who said 'Yes.' But this isn't leading you to Biscoe's address."

"It's filling in gaps," Julian smiled.

"You can imagine how lonely this house must have been for anybody like the Randalls, who kept no car. As she grew older, I think Mrs. Randall might have begun to want a little more society, but she didn't live very long; she died when her daughter was ten, and after that, Mr. Randall made it clear that I wouldn't be welcome any more. I would have liked to have kept in touch with his daughter, who was also my goddaughter, but a child of ten . . . it wasn't very easy. She was never sent to school; Mr. Randall preferred to have her taught by governesses, and all I could do was to assure myself that they were suitable and kind women who knew that I was available if they ever wanted my advice. But alas! when I was really needed, when I might really have been of some use, I was thousands of miles away. I had been sent away to the south of France to recover from an operation and I knew very little of what was going on here. I came back to find that everything was over and Mr. Randall was putting up the house for sale. His daughter—perhaps you know?—ran away and married, and although I'm sure that Mr. Randall didn't miss her or worry about her future, I think he had a feeling that people were talking about him and pointing to him as an unnatural father. That's why he went right up to Yorkshire, to be in an entirely new district. I bought the house and turned it into a school, and heard nothing of Mr. Randall or Biscoe until you mentioned them this morning."

"Then you don't know Biscoe's address?"

"No." Miss Raikes stared out of the window and appeared to be pondering. "I've one suggestion to offer you," she said at last. She rose and went to a writing table; sitting down, she wrote something on a piece of paper and handed it to Julian. "There," she said. "That's the address of a very old lady who lives not far from here; Lady Cranbrooke. I'm sending you to her because it was through her that Mr. Randall got one of his most successful governesses, a Miss du Feu. Miss du Feu was more than a governess; she also acted as Mr. Randall's housekeeper and paid the servants. She knew Biscoe very well, and would quite likely have known where he came from. Unfortunately, I haven't her address, but Lady Cranbrooke will have it, and if you don't feel that it's going in too much of a circle, I feel certain it will get you what you want in the end."

Julian glanced at the paper and Miss Raikes spoke reassuringly.

"I'm not sending you far," she said. "You can drive there in less than thirty minutes. As to Miss du Feu, although I don't know where she lives, I do know that she retired some years ago and I heard she had come back to these parts."

"You're very kind," said Julian. "I'm afraid I've taken up a lot of your time."

"Not at all; it's been a pleasure to see you. But you're not going?"

"Yes, I've kept you long enough."

"Nonsense," said Miss Raikes, with gentle firmness. "You must stay and have lunch with the school."

"Lunch with the . . . Oh, no!" besought Julian, panic-stricken.

"Of course you must," said Miss Raikes imperturbably. "It'll be good for you and it'll be good for the girls; they don't often get a chance of visitors on a nonvisiting day. Now come along and I'll show you where you may wash and brush up. This," she continued, sweeping out and leaving Julian no alternative but to follow, "is going to be a great day for the school; I don't as a rule appear in the dining room, but today I must take the headmistress' place. But they won't be as awed as they might be; they'll be too busy looking at you. In there; you have fifteen minutes before lunch. Now go along."

Julian went along. An hour and a half later, still perspiring gently, he was walking down the hill, breathing in large gulps of fortifying air. He was free.

He reached his car and drove away, thankfully leaving eighty girls behind him.

Chapter 11

IT WAS NOT difficult to find his way to the address written on the paper which Miss Raikes had given him. Julian got to Lady Cranbrooke's house and found that it stood near the road and had no drive leading to it. He parked his car beside the little wooden gate and, walking up to the front door, pressed the bell.

The door was opened by a tall, middle-aged woman who addressed him in a quiet voice.

"How do you do," she said. "You're Mr. Hurst, I think?" Julian's eyebrows went up and she smiled. "Miss Raikes rang me up and said that you were on your way. Will you come in here, please?"

She ushered him into a small room and motioned him to a chair.

"My name is Leslie, Miss Leslie," she told him. "Miss Raikes asked me to explain to you . . . there is something she felt she ought to have told you, but she didn't mention it because she felt that you had undergone a shattering ordeal and that your nerves were perhaps a little disordered."

"I had lunch at the school," said Julian. "With the school. In the school. Don't tell me that you've got eighty girls hidden away here?"

Miss Leslie smiled.

"No," she said. "No girls. Perhaps some young life would do us good here. No; what Miss Raikes asked me to explain to you was that Lady Cranbrooke is . . . not quite herself."

There was a long pause; Miss Leslie gave the visitor time to look into the implications of this piece of information.

"You mean," groped Julian at last, "you mean that she's . . . well, not quite—er—"

"You must judge for yourself," said Miss Leslie. "She is looking forward to seeing you; I've told her that you were on your way. You will find her a very gracious old lady—she is almost eighty, you know—and I think that you'll enjoy meeting her. You must remember that the life she leads here is very different from the one she used to lead when Lord Cranbrooke was alive and they were still at the castle. You will make allowances, I know."

She did not wait to find out whether Julian was prepared to make allowances or not; she had risen and was leading him upstairs. He followed with a sinking heart; lunch at a girls' school, he reflected bitterly, and the afternoon with a crazy countess. They were now, probably, on their way up to her bedroom; she would be lying on a large double bed wearing a yellow wig and looking like Miss Havisham. She would seize his hand in a crooked claw and squawk at him in a parrot voice. She would—

His fevered imaginings came to an abrupt end. He was on

the threshold of a large room. Miss Leslie, having opened the door and spoken his name, had withdrawn quietly and closed the door behind her. Julian was left, dumb with astonishment, but filled with a slowly mounting delight.

He was in a drawing room which he felt had been transported from an earlier, an infinitely lovelier setting. Beautiful rugs lay at his feet; curtains of brocade, softly rose-coloured, hung from the windows; exquisite furniture gleamed in the light of the fire. Flowers were everywhere. Standing with one hand resting on the mantelpiece, the other on the crook of a tall staff, was a white-haired woman. Immobile, expectant, erect and dignified, she made one of the most beautiful pictures Julian had ever seen. The artist in him paid tribute to his surroundings; the man in him paid homage to the woman and the beauty that still graced her. Without hesitation, Julian walked forward, took the hand she held out to him and bent and put his lips to it.

"I never did that before," he said, his eyes smiling into hers.

"You did it beautifully," she said in a voice that was still musical. "How nice to see a good-looking young man, and how refreshing to talk to one. Won't you sit down?"

They sat down and looked at one another. He felt completely at ease, with none of the feeling of being tethered that usually crept over him in the presence of the very old. He saw that she was frail, and her movements tremulous, but he had never seen anybody who looked more mistress of herself, and he recalled Miss Leslie's words with wonder and a little indignation.

Lady Cranbrooke talked and he listened and presently, when her eyes seemed to rest on him in enquiry, he pulled himself together with something of an effort, and apologized for his unheralded visit.

"Miss Raikes told me that you might be able to give me the address of somebody called Miss du Feu," he said.

Lady Cranbrooke smiled gently.

"Miss du Feu," she murmured. "Dear, dear Miss du Feu. You know her?"

"No, I've never met her, but I understand that she was governess to the daughter of a Mr. Randall."

"That is so; I got her the post myself," said Lady Cranbrooke. "But she worked too hard. She was too devoted, poor girl, and at last she made herself ill. Do you want to meet her?"

"I'd like to go and see her, if she doesn't live too far away— and I understand that she doesn't. I wonder if you would very kindly give me her address?"

"I shall certainly give it to you. I can't put my hand on it quite at once, but I shall have it brought for you. Will you very kindly press that bell beside you? Just one ring; that is for my companion. We shall ask her."

Julian pressed the bell once and a few moments later, the door opened and Miss Leslie entered the room.

"Miss Leslie," Lady Cranbrooke asked her, "can you, off-hand, remember where Miss du Feu lives?"

"Miss du Feu? I'm afraid I can't, Lady Cranbrooke, but I could go and look for your—"

"Oh, thank you, don't trouble," said Lady Cranbrooke gently. "We must ask Miss Masters. Would you very kindly ring that bell twice, Mr. Hurst?"

Miss Leslie withdrew, and Julian pressed the bell twice. When the door opened, he looked round to see Miss Masters, but he saw that it was Miss Leslie who had come into the room once more.

"Oh, Miss Masters," said Lady Cranbrooke, "I hope you weren't too busy?"

"No, of course not," said Miss Leslie.

"Then I wonder," said Lady Cranbrooke in her soft voice, "if you would kindly look through my address book and find out where Miss du Feu lives?"

"I will, certainly, Lady Cranbrooke. I think the book is in your bedroom; I'll—"

"Oh no, no!" protested Lady Cranbrooke gently. "If it's there, Millicent can fetch it. Thank you, Miss Masters."

The door closed behind Miss Leslie and Lady Cranbrooke appealed to Julian.

"Would you very kindly ring three times?" she requested. "My maid will bring me the book."

Julian rang three times; when the door opened, he saw without surprise that Miss Leslie had answered the summons. His throat tightened with a helpless pity; meeting Miss Leslie's eyes, he saw in them nothing but patience and tenderness.

"Millicent," said Lady Cranbrooke, "my address book is in my room; will you bring it to me, please?"

"Yes, m'lady."

Miss Leslie withdrew once more, and Lady Cranbrooke shook her head gently from side to side.

"She's getting old," she said. "Old, old; we're all getting old, I fear. Millicent isn't as strong as she was, either, but she's so devoted. . . . Oh, thank you!" she said, when Miss Leslie came in with the book. "One moment, Millicent; will you ask Clements to bring in tea? Mr. Hurst, you'll stay and have tea, won't you? It's very early, but I always take it at this time."

"Thank you," said Julian. "I'd like to stay, very much."

It was Miss Leslie who brought in tea, Miss Leslie who answered the summons for the butler to remove it and a footman to see him out. It was Miss Leslie who stood with him in the hall and handed him his coat.

"You were very gentle with her," she said gratefully. "I knew you would be."

Julian found it difficult to speak; his mind was still on the picture of his hostess pouring tea from lovely silver into delicate china. He remembered her long, thin old hands with their rings, the lace at her wrists.

"She's lovely," he said at last.

"Yes, she's lovely," agreed Miss Leslie. "I've been with her for more years than I can remember, and I've never seen her anything but gentle and kind."

"How long—?"

"It's difficult to say. The castle was beyond their means long before Lord Cranbrooke died. Things were getting worse; finally they became impossible. She became ill, and she was in a nursing home for some time, and the doctors said that her memory was affected. Her son came to see me and we talked things over and at last we decided to bring her back to this little house, near her oldest friends; a place small enough for me to cope with alone, but large enough to allow her to have some of her lovely things round her. We brought her back here, and here we are still, as you see us."

"Do you think she realizes—?"

"I don't know. But what would she gain by facing the truth? Why shouldn't she live, as she does, with her companion and her secretary and her maid and her butler and all the rest of them? It keeps memory green for both of us. I don't think of myself as the Gilbertian figure that I am, you know. Like her, I live in the past—that is, half of me does. I don't want to face present conditions, because I think that what's gone was so much better than what came afterwards. You wouldn't understand, of course, because you're of the new generation. You were kind to her, but one can't expect you to understand . . ."

"But I do understand," said Julian.

She looked at him for some time, and then she smiled.

"Perhaps you do," she said. "You must forgive me for not explaining matters to you fully before I took you up to her. But I—"

"I know," said Julian. "You don't have to tell me. And you were quite right and I'm very grateful to you."

"What for?"

"For letting me see the picture without distortion," said Julian. "I'll remember it all my life. Good-bye."

Chapter 12

Miss du Feu lived twenty miles from Thorley; Julian had no difficulty in finding the little town or the little house beyond it, which went by the name of Bush Cottage. Having reached it, he left the car at the roadside and stood looking over the low, wooden gate, but at first he saw no sign of a cottage. Not until he had advanced some yards along an overgrown path did he see before him glimpses of thatch and timber. The rest of Bush Cottage was invisible behind a tangle of honeysuckle, clematis, jasmine and a variety of other climbing plants that Julian was unable to name. They hung upon the little building, festooning it, swamping it.

Here and there a gap denoted a window; after some search, Julian saw what he took to be the front door, but even if it were, he thought that the journey to it would prove somewhat hazardous, for the path was by now invisible, and he would have to zigzag his way through overgrown flower beds, bramble bushes and some uninviting nettles.

His first impulse was to turn and go away. He had come too far already from any hope of contact with Alexandra. He had been foolish to leave London, foolish to waste time at Holside and Thorley. He was glad to have seen Lady Cranbrooke, but he regretted having pursued his investigations further. It had seemed reasonable enough, in Mr. Stevens' shop, to talk of setting out to find Biscoe's address, but it had proved a useless journey. It had ended here, in this wilderness; he was looking at a garden that was lost, like himself, a house that was entangled, like his thoughts and a path that had ended in nothingness. There was nothing to be gained by wasting his time in interviewing a governess who would no doubt prove to be as creeper-clad as her cottage.

He turned the matter over in his mind: back over the path to his car, or on through the obstacles to the front door. As he was debating, a voice spoke from a bush nearby with a suddenness that made him jump.

"Good afternoon," it said briskly. "Are you looking for me?"

Julian turned in the general direction of the sound.

"I'm looking for Miss du Feu," he said.

"Ah! I'm Miss du Feu. I'll be with you in just a moment," promised the voice. "Can you see me?"

"No," said Julian, promptly and unhesitatingly. If this was another unhinged hostess playing at I Spy, the sooner he leapt into his car and drove off, the better it would be. But he hesitated, for there was nothing unhinged about the voice, and the figure that emerged from the undergrowth a moment later was sturdy and sensible-looking and with nothing in the least deranged about it. A first glance told him that although Miss de Feu's clothes would have looked in place on a stall

171

at a Jumble sale, her bearing had dignity; more, it had authority.

"Here I am," she announced, coming up to him. "How do you do? How nice it is to see you; I have very few visitors."

"I just came," began Julian, "to—"

But Miss du Feu had held up a hand, and he fell silent, as a score of misses had fallen silent upon seeing the commanding gesture.

"We shall go indoors," stated Miss du Feu. "This isn't the kind of afternoon for outdoor meetings; that wind is far too strong. Will you follow me? There used to be a path, but time stole it, foot by foot. To find it again now would take something in the nature of excavations, I imagine."

Julian murmured in reply, but his whole attention was focused upon his hostess' appearance, and he found it difficult to attend to what she was saying. He was following her, and so could indulge his curiosity and stare as much as he wanted to, and he found much to make him stare.

Miss du Feu was rather short, but the set of her shoulders and the soldierly stiffness of her walk added a good deal to her height. Her hair was grey and she wore it in loops over her ears; she had on a short tweed jacket, a thick woolen skirt and a pair of stout boots. Julian could not guess her age, but he put it in the sixties, noting as he did so that there was nothing elderly about Miss du Feu's walk or bearing. She was still talking, flinging sentences over her shoulder as she went.

"Fifteen years ago," she said, "this place looked well cared for. I thought I could keep it looking like that, but I found that two hands and two feet and the will to work were not enough to pit against the encroachments of nature. I can't employ labour; I tried it once, but it made no appreciable difference to anything except my purse, don't you know. So I had to do without all that expensive assistance, and when I die—which I hope won't be for a great many years yet—perhaps there will be people here with the strength and the time to make the place look pretty again. Here we are now. Mind the step, will you? It's—oh, I should have told you earlier. Did you hurt yourself?"

Julian, lurching against the wall of the narrow passage into which he had stumbled, assured her that he was unhurt. He followed her into a little room, and she closed the door and drew up two chairs.

"Do sit down, will you?" she invited. "This is a very general sort of room. It's by way of being a living room. I eat in here."

It was evident to Julian that Miss du Feu did more than eat in there; he could see that she slept, ironed, mended, cooked, swept, dusted, grew bulbs, mixed chicken food and dog food, washed, read, wrote and listened to the radio in there. Living room, he thought, summed it up very nicely.

"Now"—His hostess settled herself in her chair and looked at him expectantly—"tell me, please, who you are and why you came to see me."

"My name's Hurst, Julian Hurst. I came—"

He stopped. Miss du Feu had clapped her hands to her cheeks and was staring at him with her eyes staring and startled.

"*Tell* me," she besought in an agitated voice, "do tell me—did I leave that *poor* animal outside?"

"I—" Julian's expression denoted his complete lack of understanding.

"That *unfortunate* dog," explained Miss du Feu. "He *hates* to be forgotten—but I came in, my mind full of other matters, and I shut the door, it may be, right in his poor faithful face. Do, I beg you, like a good boy, do go and see if he's outside on the doorstep."

Julian rose and threaded a way to the door. Going out into the passage and negotiating the step, this time without mishap, he opened the front door. Outside, one of the dogs he had seen on his arrival was sitting in an attitude of outraged dignity; on seeing the door open, he rose, gave Julian a cold look and walked past him without thanks into the living room.

"Oh, *thank* you," said Miss du Feu, on Julian's return. "That was so kind! The dogs understand that I can't think of everything, but sometimes they do feel a little reproachful. Now, you were saying—"

"It was something in connection with a Mr. Randall," said Julian.

"Mr. Randall? Mr. Matthew Randall?" enquired Miss du Feu.

"Yes."

Miss du Feu's eyes became distant and dreamy.

"Mr. Randall," she said, in a slow and musing tone. "After all these years—to hear of him." She shook herself out of a reverie and gave her attention to Julian once more. "I was governess to his daughter, you know."

"Yes, but it was really—"

"May I interrupt you for a moment to ask whether you're a friend of Mr. Randall's?" asked Miss du Feu.

"No, I'm not. In any case, he died a short while ago."

"I'm glad," said Miss du Feu. "Not glad that he died, of course, unless he was suffering and it was a happy release, but glad that you weren't a friend of his, because he was a rather horrid man."

"Yes, I heard so. I only met him twice."

"He was a selfish man and a bad father," said Miss du Feu, dropping her voice with a view, perhaps, to keeping the damaging facts from the Recording Angel. "He was self-absorbed and oblivious to his duty. But his daughter was the most charming young girl who ever came under my care: gentle, warm-hearted and full of spirit. She was made for a full, happy life, and he kept her shut up, not shut up in the fairy-story sense, you understand, but shut away from everything that a young girl needs—young people of her own age, parties, gaiety and fun, even young men, though she was a little young for that sort of thing when I was with her. That great house, right up on the hill, and no car—no transport of any kind, and no station nearby. It was all very nice for Mr. Randall, of course, and nothing would induce him to consider his daughter's needs. She had governess after governess; none of them would stay, of course, because the place offered nothing in the way of change or relaxation."

"Ah," said Julian, vaguely. "Well, what I was—"

"I should tell you at once that I stayed as long as my health allowed me to. Mr. Randall did his best to get rid of me, but I was much too experienced to give him any just cause for dismissing me. I spoke my mind to him, not once, but many times, and of course he didn't like that, but I was all that he could ask as a guardian for his daughter, and so he couldn't send me away."

"Ah, yes," said Julian. "Well, I—"

"I should never have gone if I hadn't become ill," proceeded Miss du Feu steadily. "I would have stayed and I would certainly have got her away, eventually, from that cloistered life, and out into the world. But when I was fit for work again, and that wasn't for over two years, I found that she had very sensibly done that for herself. I suppose you know that she has been dead for many years?"

"Yes, I— But it wasn't really about Mr. Randall or his daughter that I came to see you. It was about a butler, it was—"

"Biscoe!" cried Miss du Feu, bringing her palm down with a resounding smack on the table that separated her from her guest. "Biscoe, dear old Biscoe! Don't tell me that the dear old man is *still* alive?"

"Yes. That is, he was two or three months ago."

"Dear, dear, dear me!" mused Miss du Feu. "And he didn't look as though he'd last out the year, the last time I saw him. Dear old Biscoe! Never, never could he get hold of my name; he always called me Miss Doofer. What a devoted servant he was!"

"Yes, he seemed to be."

"Seemed! He was *part* of the Randalls. He had no life away or apart from them. What *would* have killed him at once, of course, would have been the necessity of choosing between one or other of them: Mr. Randall or his wife, or Mr. Randall or his daughter. But the decision was never called for; Mrs. Randall died very early in his service and he stayed with Mr. Randall and his daughter; when Miss Randall left home, there was no question of her taking Biscoe with her, and so he remained with Mr. Randall, I suppose, to the end."

"Yes."

"And I don't need to ask whether he received any kind of pension, because I knew his master too well to waste any words on questions of that kind. He left Biscoe, I'm sure, totally unprovided for?"

"Yes." Julian saw an opportunity and used it at once. "That's why I want to trace him," he said.

"Trace him?"

"To trace Biscoe. I ought to explain that my father's firm acted for Mr. Randall. After his death, nobody thought of finding out where Biscoe lived, and so he left without any provision having been made for him. I was directed to you as someone who might have known where he came from."

"He came from London," said Miss du Feu at once, "but I don't imagine that that's much use, to you."

"Don't you know whereabouts in London?"

"I'm most terribly sorry, but—" Miss du Feu's hands went up to her cheeks and her eyes bulged alarmingly. "My dear boy!" she said in distraught tones, "did I—did I put that cover on?"

"Cover?"

"Out at the back, and to the left. The cover of the rain barrel," explained the agitated Miss du Feu. "I get *nightmares!* Those kittens *will* jump up and walk along the edge and once, when I first came here"— Miss du Feu closed her eyes and a shudder shook her solid frame—"No, I can't speak of it. Do run and look, there's a good boy!"

Julian went, but at a walk. The cover was off, and he replaced it and returned to his hostess, who beamed at him in gratitude.

"That was very kind," she said. "You mustn't think me careless; when I'm alone, which as a rule I am, I have my little system of doing this and that, but if my mind is taken off by anything untoward—not that your visit is untoward; it's charming and the very sight of a nice young man like you has cheered me up immensely—but it does tend to make me forget this and that. Now we must go back to Biscoe. London. You're looking for one poor old man out of all the thousands of poor old men in the vast city of London, and you came to me for help, and I've given you none. But you see, when I went to the Randalls, he was already an institution; he had been engaged long, long ago in the dim past; he had been in their service long before I went to them and although he went off, once or twice during my time there, to visit what I understood to be his only remaining relative in London, I never thought—never dreamed—of asking where he lived."

"Did he ever mention the district, or say anything that would have given some idea of—"

"No, nothing," said Miss du Feu. "But there *is* one thing, though I don't promise it will lead to anything. I could get it for you—you must give me a little time, because I should have to look through my papers—I could find for you the address at which Mr. Randall's daughter lived in London."

"Thank you," said Julian, without enthusiasm. "It's very kind of you, but I don't feel that—"

"It *might* help, you know," said Miss du Feu. "Did it not occur to you that your best hope of finding Biscoe is through the Randalls? I always kept in touch with Miss Randall, you know, before and after her marriage. I meant more to her, I think, than her father ever did. I'll find the address for you —I ought to know it without looking, but my memory isn't what it was. I'll find it for you, if you give me a moment."

Julian felt that there was no real need for him to argue or protest: Miss du Feu had gone to a desk which was almost lost under a miscellaneous collection of papers, ornaments and crockery, and was pulling out drawers and rummaging in them.

"I'll find it," she said with confidence. "It might take me a little time. Sometimes, when I'm looking for something else,

I come across old letters and read them and then I forget—"
She broke off and turned to face Julian and he saw with dismay that her face was wearing the now familiar look of panic.
"*Did* I," she moaned, "*did* I . . . *do* you think I put them out?"

"Put—?"

"The eggs! I sell them, you know. I put them into a basket and leave them beside the gate and the bus stops and picks them up and takes them in, but if I don't put them out in full view, then the driver knows there aren't any and so he doesn't stop; he goes whizzing straight by and—oh dear me! *Could* you—? *Would* you just peep out into the passage and see if there's a basket full of eggs just by— There *is?* Oh my goodness! Run, run, *run,* like a good boy and you may just catch him. *Fly!* Oh fly! Mind the loose stones by the— oh, you *poor* boy! Hurry, hurry . . ."

Her voice was lost in the distance; Julian was doing a combination obstacle and egg-and-spoon race to the gate, spurred by the sound of a heavy vehicle that was coming nearer and nearer. He reached the gate, threw it open, saw the bus as it went by, and yelled with all the strength of his lungs. The driver may or may not have heard the sound, but there was no mistaking the familiar basket that was being waved in the air. The bus slowed, and Julian raced up the road and handed the basket to a pleasant-faced country woman who reached out to take it. Breathless with haste and some of Miss du Feu's panic, he turned and walked to the cottage and found his way back to the living room.

"Now, that was a work of mercy," said Miss du Feu approvingly, as he entered. "Those eggs go straight to the hospital. From hen to hospital within an hour or two; if it hadn't been for you, all those poor patients would have missed their

179

brand-new-laid eggs today. I'm getting on, as you see. While I'm doing this, why don't you make us both some tea?"

Julian, circling round this request and finding no way out of it, rose and did his best to look as though making tea was part of his daily routine.

"The tea is in that tin with the birds on it," directed Miss du Feu over her shoulder. "Milk in the brown jug on the mantelpiece over there and sugar . . . where? Oh, there! Just move that bowl of fruit—there. Water . . . I'm afraid you'll have to get that from the pump outside, unless—how much is there in the kettle?"

"Quite enough," said Julian firmly. "Now if you just tell me what to do, I'll do it while you go on looking."

Following his hostess' directions, he made and served two cups of tea, and Miss du Feu came over and sat with him at the table and produced some biscuits which she placed between them. They ate and drank with—on Julian's part—a growing sense of comfort; Miss du Feu was an oddity, but there was, all the same, something about her that he greatly liked.

"People call me odd," she said, as though following his thoughts, "but I'm not really odd at all—except in having imagined that I could run a place like this entirely on my own. It was what I had always dreamed of; it's what all governesses always used to dream of when they had got over dreaming about a husband and children: a little cottage of their own. But I had to have it all: the cottage, the chickens, the dogs and cats, the garden with its flowers and plenty of vegetables, the cosy little room with a warm fire crackling away in winter. Well, it's all here, and I'm very fortunate and very grateful and very happy, but I can only do what I *can* do, and I can't afford to employ labour. I do what I can myself, and very little it comes to compared with what *ought* to be done. I need a gardener and a daily maid and handyman now and again, but I can't have them. If I could, the place would look trim and well-cared-for and everybody would come and see me and talk of me as that charming woman who used to be governess to Lord Wallertree's daughters and the Countess of Sharbrook's nieces. People used to come once, but I noticed that as the hedges began to look neglected, the list grew shorter; then the path became overgrown and the bushes got out of hand the pretty flower beds vanished one by one—just vanished. All that digging, all that planting, all that tending . . . whoosh! vanished! and so had the visitors, and I was really rather relieved, on the whole, because most visitors give as much bother as pleasure, don't you know—except nice young men like you, who help me so much and make such good tea!"

Julian smiled at her, but there was no need for him to speak. Miss du Feu's eyes had become misty and her voice was dreamy with reminiscence.

"You've taken me back a great many years," she said. "Miss Randall was such a dear girl. Thank God I was still vigorous enough to be a real companion to her; we walked, we even ran, and we laughed—dear me, how we laughed, though I can't remember what we laughed at. You would have said, wouldn't you, that a girl brought up as she had been—with no young people of her own age, with a selfish and uninterested father—would have grown sad and dull and melancholy. But no! She had the sunniest disposition of any girl I ever had under my charge; *nothing* could quench her happy spirit, thank God. Not even her painting, though most of it was enough to depress anybody; she *tried*, you know, but she really had no talent. Sometimes I wondered if I ought to discourage her, but I didn't, and what a good thing I didn't! Because it was her painting that brought her, in the end, to happiness. If I hadn't encouraged her, if I hadn't forced her father, after long and bitter battles, to allow her to have a good teacher . . . She didn't have one while I was there, and so I never saw him. She kept her father to his bargain, however, and when she was eighteen, he did allow a teacher to come to the house and— What did you say?"

Julian was staring at her. He was trying to piece something together in his mind. Miss Randall, her painting, her painting master . . . her husband . . . Clauval. Clauval! His voice was eager as he addressed Miss du Feu.

"Miss Randall's husband . . . Was he—he wasn't by any chance a Frenchman, was he?" he asked.

"Dear me, no," said Miss du Feu. "I shouldn't have encouraged Mr. Randall to have a Frenchman in the house, and I'm sure he wouldn't have agreed to it. No, no. He was as English as you or I—you *are* English, I take it, and not Scottish or— Yes, well, so was he. I never saw him, I regret to say, though I had invitations enough to go and stay with them in London when they were married. He was a thoroughly good young man; I wouldn't trust his wife's estimate of him if it weren't borne out by his behaviour. He was engaged by Mr. Randall and he went to stay in the house, and the lessons—there were to be twelve of them—began under the eye of my most excellent successor. The two young people fell in love—instantly and deeply and lastingly. He went to Mr. Randall and in the most straightforward way asked for his daughter's hand, and Mr. Randall's answer was to tell Biscoe to throw him out of the house—a thing poor Biscoe couldn't have attempted even if he'd agreed to such a course. There was nothing against the match except the young man's poverty; he had no money and no expectations; all he had was his genius—it is his wife's word—as a painter."

"Did they run away?"

"Certainly not," said Miss du Feu. "There was no hole-and-corner behaviour. They declared that they would marry; Mr. Randall promised—and they both knew he would keep his promise—to disinherit his daughter absolutely. They went to London and they were married from my sister's house at Putney and the fact that I can't recall her married name at once makes me realize that my memory isn't what it was. And now I'll go back to my search while you just take the cups out, if you will, and just sloosh them in that little basin I keep by the rain barrel—only you will remember, won't you, to put the cover on again?"

He went out and slooshed the cups and as he slooshed, he looked round and contrasted his lot with that of Miss du Feu's and wondered, whether, after all, his muscles got all the exercise they needed in his shop in Kensington, and whether one man alone—or one young man with one young woman—could keep a cottage like this in good repair and stop the flower beds from vanishing and the hedges from overgrowing and the bushes from getting out of hand. For the first time in his life, he studied himself in a setting that was green and open and unbounded. He moved a little in the frame, and set Alexandra beside him, and stared into the future and wondered . . . and wondered . . .

A jubilant cry from inside the house brought him back to the present. He turned to see Miss du Feu standing in the back door and saw that in her hand she held several letters. She waved them at him in triumph and spoke in a tone of triumph.

"Got it!" she declared. "All her dear letters; I shall keep

183

them out and reread them by the fire tonight. A great joy for me, but not very much, perhaps for you. However, here's the address. I shall write it down for you."

Julian picked up the two cups and saucers and prepared to follow her into the house.

"And the name?" he asked.

"Oh yes, the name. Naturally, you'll want the name too. I can't *think* how I ever forgot it, but you must bring those cups and come inside and we'll write it down."

"What is it?" asked Julian.

"She married a man called Bell," said Miss du Feu, "and they had the sweetest little daughter called— Oh! Well never mind; they didn't belong to a set, you know, and you can replace them very cheaply at Woolworth's. If you'll just pick up the pieces, like a good boy, I'll show you where to put them."

Chapter 13

"IF ONLY YOU'D *told* me!" repeated Miss du Feu, for perhaps the tenth time.

She was seated beside Julian in his car, and they were going towards London at a speed which, though excessive, appeared to affect neither Miss du Feu's nerves nor her hat. Her nerves seemed to be unshakable; her hat was anchored firmly by means of a gauze veil that was draped over it and fastened under her chin.

"If you'd only *asked*, my dear Julian! How extraordinary of you to come and ask me for information about Biscoe, when I was the one person in the world—if you'd only realized, had you had your wits about you—the one person who could lead you at once to Alexandra. Was it likely that I—I!—who had loved her mother, who had given her mother such care, such affection—would I lose touch with her daughter? Was it likely that—dear me! are we through Honiton

185

already? I suppose there were notices saying that one mustn't drive at more than thirty miles an hour, but when one is going at this rate, one can declare with perfect truth that one didn't see them. To think, Julian, that you wasted all that time talking to me about extraneous matters when I might have been telling you about Alexandra."

"I'd made up my mind that Biscoe was the one to look for."

"The fixed idea again; how it misleads us! I used to warn all my girls against that very thing, and you see how right I was! Julian, you are *quite* certain that Mr. Gosse will go and feed my hens?"

"Quite certain."

"I shouldn't have come away in this impulsive fashion, but the temptation was too much! I haven't been able to afford a trip to London for years, and the thought of seeing Alexandra again after all this time . . . But I can't think what my sister will say when I arrive at her house in Putney, when I descend upon her suddenly in this way . . . You did say we should stop on the way and let me telephone to her."

"Yes, we'll do it later."

"She'll be very glad to see me. She never visits me; she says that my house—she has a very joking sort of way with her—gives her the creepers. I suppose it would be too late for you to come in and meet her when we get to the house?"

"I'm afraid so. You were saying that Alexandra—"

"I first saw her when she was four," said Miss du Feu, "and dear me, how pretty she was! She got her looks from her father, of course. Her mother was beautiful within but not, by accepted standards, without. But you can understand what fascination she had when I tell you that her husband loved her from the moment his eyes fell on her. She often used to tell me about it; he was so handsome, she said, and so— Was that Yeovil?"

"Probably. Go on."

"Love at first sight. That may sound too romantic, but in this case, it really did happen. And they were happy . . . so happy, but of course you know that he died when Alexandra was three?"

"Yes."

"I never saw him, I regret to say. It was in another situation in a far corner of Wales, and I couldn't get away for visits to London. But when I heard of his death, I handed in my resignation and went immediately . . . but there was so little I could do for her. But it was then that I learned for the first time about Clauval, and when I heard the whole story, I knew how much he must have loved her. You can picture it all, can't you? The young artist engaged to go to a house and teach a young lady; he arrives and I don't doubt that while he was in the drawing room waiting for her to come downstairs, he takes the opportunity of looking at some of her paintings. His heart sinks; no talent. No real talent. He had much better tell her, or tell her father or her governess, that he will only be wasting his time—and the young lady's. Can't you see him thinking that?"

"Yes. Go on."

"So just as he has made up his mind to be frank, she comes into the room. And he finds that he can't be as frank as he had thought. And so the lessons begin, and by way of showing her, teaching her, he paints the first head: the *Green Girl*. By the time the last one, the *Silver Girl*, is done, they know that they are in love. They know that, come what may, they will be married. She told me that from the first they never had any real hope of her father's agreeing; the

187

first question he would ask would be about prospects—and what prospects has a young and penniless artist? But she said that she was sure they could live by selling their pictures. Their pictures . . . not his pictures, you see. Because he never, to the end, brought himself to tell her the truth. From the very beginning, she thought of them as working together, of being one. And so those four pictures were signed with their joint names: Claud and Valentine. Clauval came into being, and now you know why there were two different Clauvals. He was the real, the good Clauval, and poor Valentine, poor, poor Valentine—"

"When did she find out?"

"Not until after his death. The dealers she went to told her the truth with far less kindness or pity than Claud would have done. She learned that her own work had never had the slightest value, and she suspected that she had ruined his chances of making a name for himself by producing, as he would have done by himself, work of unvarying merit. She learned too late to remedy the evil, but the knowledge of her husband's love and his desire to shield her . . . you can understand how much it helped her in the struggle that came afterwards."

"He ought to have told her; after all, they had a daughter to support."

"Yes . . . but when they married, Valentine was eighteen and Claud was twenty-six. If there is a young man of twenty-six who can bring himself to tell his young wife that her paintings are worthless, I hope I may never meet him."

"Wouldn't old Randall—"

"Never. You saw him; would you have gone to him to beg?"

"To provide for Alexandra, I would."

188

"Well, you would have gone in vain. I went to him again and again. Biscoe pleaded for them, and it was all quite useless. He simply took the view that what he had was his daughter's, until she rejected it. She had chosen for herself; he had told her that if she married a man he considered to be nothing but a fortune-hunter, she could expect nothing further from him financially, either then or at his death. There was nothing ranting or melodramatic about it, you know; it was just cold-blooded reasoning. He didn't see why he should accept a man who was, he was quite convinced, only after her money. Sometimes I have a dreadful feeling that he almost forgot Valentine. He had no imagination; he wouldn't have been able to picture her in want or poverty. Her husband had stated that he would keep her; let him do so. Poor little Valentine!"

"Were they happy?"

"Of course. Alexandra has her mother's temperament—can you imagine Alexandra miserable?"

"No."

"Well, then. Alexandra has all her mother's lightness of heart, but thank God, she also has her father's courage. Yes, they were happy. When Claud died, I went to Mr. Randall for the last time. He behaved as though he'd never had a daughter or a granddaughter, and I knew that he would never make provision for either of them. But Valentine, once she turned from painting, found that she had practical gifts which would help her to earn money. Alexandra grew up as useful and practical as Valentine had learned to be, and when Valentine died, and I came to London to see what Alexandra was going to do—she was only sixteen, you know—I found that I had no need to worry about her. She was already at work, and she has been at work ever since. She has earned her own living far more competently, and in far more ways, than I was ever able to. And she deserves a far better fate than to be abandoned by a young man who—"

"I didn't abandon her."

"Oh yes, you did. If you'd had the slightest intuition, you would have known what your desertion meant to a sensitive girl like Alexandra. She— Isn't that the spire of Salisbury Cathedral?"

"Probably. Am I going too fast for you?"

"For me? For me, no," said Miss du Feu. "For safety, perhaps; for the police, undoubtedly. It's most interesting to see how different these places look when they flash by like this. I can scarcely recognize them, and yet I know them all so well. But you're not really listening to me; your eyes are on the road and your mind is on Alexandra. I'm interested to hear she was a cook; she has done a great many things, but she didn't tell me that she had ever worked as a cook. I wonder if we might stop and telephone to my sister?"

"We'll do it from Guildford."

"Very well. Do you think that Mr. Gosse will remember to give the dogs—"

"Sure do," said Julian, and then, to his own and Miss du Feu's astonishment, raised his voice and broke into loud and cheerful song. He had not sung since New Year's Eve, but his joy was too great to contain.

She was found. The search was over. She was found ... almost. She was his . . . almost. He would deliver Miss du Feu into her sister's care and then he would go to the address that she had given him; there, where Alexandra's father and mother had lived, there, at Number 13 Abbess Avenue, Pimlico, there would he find Alexandra. He knew who she was and where she was; other explanations could

190

wait until he held her in his arms. The pictures. . . . It was no use mentioning them to Miss du Feu except to tell her, as he had told her, that Mr. Randall had given them to him to take to London. Alexandra herself would have to explain why she had chosen to hide herself and put him to so much worry and so much trouble—and so much expense.

He thought, with an unexpected sense of pride, of his home. He pictured it, as he drove, and saw its wide front door open to admit Alexandra as he led her in. He visualized his mother's pleasure and his father's surprise. It would take the old man some time to figure out the train of events that had led to her entry into the family, but no doubt, thought Julian, he would get there in time. Nannie would not bother to get there at all, except to tell him that he ought to have found her years before, you great ninny, you. Drusilla would be too full of her coming journey out to Cuffy to do more than note that Alexandra was even prettier than she was; Oliver would talk to him about family responsibilities and Madeleine would see to it that no detail of his past exploits failed to reach the ears of his fiancée. Alexandra would become one of them. They would marry—where? Same as Oliver and Madeleine, he supposed. They would live—where? Somewhere fairly near town. Chelsea? Too low, too near the river. Hampstead? Too high and too far out. Knightsbridge? Too expensive. Belgravia? Not bad, one of those really well-converted Mews places. They would take their time. Furniture? Aunt Rowena would want to make herself heard; she liked to pretend that she knew a genuine antique when she saw one. Silver, linen, china, glass. . . . It had a steady, a satisfying beat, a rhythm—silver, linen, china, glass; Eeeny, meeny, miney, mo; silver, linen, china, glass; silver, linen, china, glass . . . a home for Alexandra.

A home for Alexandra, who had never had a real home . . . who had only had a small and inadequate piece of Number 13 Abbess Avenue, Pimlico. A home for Alexandra and himself. And their children; no, perhaps he'd better not think about their children now, as he was coming into the thick traffic of London.

He stopped at a house in Putney and delivered Miss du Feu into a dimly lit hall and the care of a long woolen dressing gown and something which his mother identified for him later as a boudoir cap. The oddness of the outfit was explained when Miss du Feu, seeing him off at the door, explained that her sister always went to bed at ten-thirty and it was now after midnight. This surprising piece of information recalled Julian to a sense of time and made him realize that this was a somewhat unsuitable hour for an assault upon Abbess Avenue. He would go in the morning. He would go at dawn. He would wake up Pimlico by standing outside the house and shouting for Alexandra. Come out, come out, my sweet . . . that ought to go down well in that neighbourhood at six-thirty on a nice spring morning.

He got to Campden Hill and entered the hall to find his mother on her way upstairs to bed. He took her in his arms and kissed her lightly on the tip of her nose. She looked at him with a smile.

"There's no need to ask," she said. "You've found her."

"I have. Did Aunt Rowena tell you about her?"

"She told me what you told her. Julian, my dear, can she really cook?"

"She can really cook."

"Is she pretty?"

"She's lovely." They were in the drawing room. "She's—"

He stopped, and his mother, after waiting for him to finish his sentence, spoke in a tone of pleading.

"Do go on, Julian! We've waited all these weeks thinking that somebody had—what's the word?—spurned you. We thought you were—"

"—nursing a broken heart. Well, not exactly. I was worried, that's all."

"Where did you find her?"

"I haven't really found her yet. I just know where she is, that's all. I'm going to see her tomorrow—today. And that's all I'm going to tell you until I bring her to you, Mother darling."

"But why dole it out piecemeal? She's pretty, she's useful and you're going to marry her. That's something, but there's such a lot more! Her name, her address, her parents, where you met her, why you were worried, why you went away, and where—do talk in long, comprehensive, informative sentences and fill in all the gaps. I've been very patient, you know."

"You've been wonderful, and I'm damn grateful. But Mother, I'm going to see her today. She's got a good deal of explaining to do herself. I'll get it all out of her and then I'll bring her round to you and give you a nice, complete, rounded-off story with a happy-ever-after ending. I'm going round at dawn and I'll—"

"If you think that getting a girl of—how old is she?"

"Twenty-two."

"—of twenty-two out of bed in the morning without giving her time to put her make-up on and get the pins out of her hair, you—"

"Pins?"

"Why not? She must have the usual sort of hair that wants keeping in the usual sort of order."

"She doesn't sleep in pins."

"Really?"

"Really. But don't run away with any wild ideas. And don't ask questions. Tomorrow—today—I'll lead her in, as I swore I'd do the first time I saw her. No, the second time. She put my program a bit out of gear, but there's no reason why I shouldn't carry it out now. I said I'd lead her in and I'm damn well going to lead her in, if I have to drag her by the hair. Mother, is there anything to eat? I'm starving."

"Come along into the kitchen and I'll get you something. Haven't you had any food lately?"

"I had lunch with eighty girls, tea with a beautiful countess and some more tea with a governess."

"That's quite a day. But even you must have found eighty girls a little overpowering, surely?"

"You'll be careful tomorrow, won't you, Mother, about things like that 'even you'?"

"I'll try. Shall I cut these crusts off?"

"No. Leave them."

"Will you mix some mustard?"

"I sat next to Miss Raikes," said Julian, mixing vigorously.

"That's interesting," said his mother. "Is this girl of yours cooking for a living, or is she one of these new cookery-school graduates doing it, as it were, between school and getting married?"

"She's doing it for a living. She's been working since she was sixteen. Mother—"

"Well?"

"We've got an awful lot to sort of make up to her for."

His mother pondered this involved statement while he ate, and then made a quiet observation.

"I don't know who or what she is," she said, "but I can tell you something, and that is that she's done something to you."

"Of course she has." Julian's mouth was full, but the words came out with reasonable clearness. "Of course she has. She's changed my entire life."

"She's done something that I was never able to do," pursued his mother.

"What's that?" enquired Julian.

"She's done for you what Cuffy did for Drusilla."

"Ho? What was that?"

"I can't put it into words; well, I could, but it would sound a little harsh. What I mean is that both you and Drusilla had too much of something—self-confidence, perhaps—and now you've got a good deal less of it, and it suits you both a good deal better. I hope I make myself clear?"

"Perfectly; we've both had the stuffing knocked out of us."

"Stuffing," mused Mrs. Hurst. "It wasn't quite the word I was after."

"It'll do," said Julian. "Not that I'm agreeing with you, mark *you*. I grant you that Drusilla doesn't throw her weight around half as much as she used to, but marriage does that to some girls."

"It does that to some men too, fortunately," said Mrs. Hurst. "Do you want coffee?"

"Not coffee," said Julian, after consideration. "I'd like a nice big cup of nice strong cocoa, made with all milk and lashings of sugar, topped with a bit of cream. I'll take it up to bed with me. How's the family?"

"It's nice of you to remember them. They're all very well,

thank you. Your father's still talking of retiring. Rowena says business is brisk. The baby's put on weight; Drusilla's got a nurse to take out with her."

"That's expensive, isn't it?"

"Fairly, but Cuffy's mother insisted."

"She who insisteth, payeth, I trust," said Julian.

"Madeleine came round today with some good news. She's going to have another baby in August."

"I hope Oliver thinks that's good news."

"He's delighted."

"I suppose Madeleine and Drusilla'll be taking turn and turn about for the next who-knows-how-many years?"

"Perhaps; it might even become a three-cornered contest," pointed out his mother.

"There! You've made me burn my tongue!" said Julian.

"If you've finished, go upstairs quietly," said Mrs. Hurst. "Your father might be just going off to sleep and I don't want him disturbed. And don't think of going round to your mysterious young woman before half-past nine or ten o'clock. Then she'll be up and dressed, with a good breakfast inside her."

"Only toast and coffee; that's all she likes. What are you smiling at?"

"The thought of your father telling somebody—before he and I were even engaged—that I didn't sleep with my hair in pins and that I only took toast and coffee for breakfast. These are odd times, you know. Don't you young people ever leave yourselves any surprises?"

"I'm going to be married; that's one big surprise," said Julian, bending to kiss her while balancing a cup of cocoa in his hand. "Sorry to keep you guessing for just one more night."

"That's all right; joy—and enlightenment, no doubt—cometh in the morning. Put the light out as you go. Shall I bring you up a cup of tea in the morning?"

"Would you?"

"Yes, but I won't bring it too early. Go up and have a nice long sleep and I'll wake you at about eight."

He went up and slept, but not soundly. Girls in green skirts and white blouses waited upon him with cups of thick, creamy chocolate; Miss Raikes, meeting him as he hurried down a steep hill, thrust a basket of eggs into his hands and begged him to take them to the castle and give them to Mrs. Cole. He tossed restlessly, for he was struggling with frenzied haste out of a tail coat and striped trousers, and donning a footman's livery. He was at a rain barrel, fishing kittens out of the water and wrapping them in scarlet cloaks to keep them warm. He was driving, driving down an endless road, and Dr. Glitter, seated beside him, was wearing a hat with a gauze veil tied under his chin. He saw a house ahead, but although he drove faster and faster, it seemed to get no nearer; then he saw that it was Holside Manor. He got out and walked up to it and rang the bell: one for the companion, two for the secretary, three for . . .

He woke with a start. His mother had put a tray on the table beside him and was sitting on his bed and shaking him gently.

"Eight o'clock," she said.

He lay staring up at her drowsily.

"Is her name Raikes?" asked Mrs. Hurst.

"No. Why?"

"I've been listening to you. Is she Glitter?"

"No."

"That's a relief. Is she Cranbrooke?"

"Good Lord, have I been through all that? No, she isn't."

"That's an even greater relief. Anthea?"

"No. I seem to have had a nice, sociable night."

"You sounded quite fevered." She rose. "Well, good luck, Julian. Do you want me to smarten myself up, or had she better see me without the trimmings?"

"No trimmings."

"May I talk shop to her, as it were? She might tell me what I do wrong with rissoles."

"Do I need a haircut?"

"She won't notice. Call out when you're on your way down, will you? I'm making omelettes for breakfast."

She left Julian to drink his tea, and as he did so, as he had his bath, as he shaved and dressed, his spirits rose higher and higher. He was going to see her, soon, today, in an hour or two . . .

His distracted frame of mind made his dressing a longer business than it usually was; when he went down to breakfast, it was to find that his father had left for the office. Julian was not sorry; he had nothing to say as yet, and his father's breakfast-time observations were not as a rule of marked interest.

"Have you seen Drusilla?" his mother asked him.

"Not yet; if she isn't down before I go, I'll go up and tell her the baby's a marvel."

He finished his breakfast and stood up, and a wave of joyous anticipation swept over him. Waiting was over; worry was over; in a short while he would hold Alexandra in his arms. Whatever he had done wrong, however he had failed her . . . all would be forgotten when they met.

He began to whistle—a high, piercing, ear-shattering sound that made his mother smile in the kitchen. Travelling up to the floor above, the sound caused the baby to break into roars of protest. Julian, whistling his way across the hall and upstairs to see his nephew, heard the yells and switched from the popular air he had begun, to the twitter and chirrup of birds—sounds designed to turn the infant mind to thoughts of the peaceful countryside. Then an ever shriller sound fell on his ears, and he turned and went downstairs again to answer the summons of the telephone.

"I'll get it, Mother," he yelled. "Oh—sorry, I thought you were in the kitchen."

"I was, and I will be again," said Mrs. Hurst. "Do you have to make that dreadful noise?"

"Mother, I do." Julian lifted the receiver. "Hello, hello, hello, hello? This is— Oh, it's you, Oliver. Good morning, good morning, superlatively good morning. What are you doing at the office, nose upon grindstone, on this the first, the very first day of May? This, brother, is a day of revelry. This is the merrie month—remember?"

"If you'll stop clowning," said Oliver's voice, with a grave note in it that Julian knew well, "perhaps I can get some sense out of you. For God's sake, what was that noise?"

"I just whistled. I'm sorry. But this is my big day. I'm just off to meet my fiancée. F-i-a-n-c and two e's to show how feminine she is. What did you say?"

"I said that you will go nowhere—nowhere, you understand?—until you've come down to the office and cleared up something here."

"Later," said Julian.

"You'll come now," said Oliver, "and you'll come soon, or I'll go straight in to see Father, and I'll inform him that you've been mixed up in some shady dealing connected with old Mr. Randall."

"Oh, come, come, *come!*" protested Julian. "Them's hard words."

"I have a man here in the office," pursued Oliver, "and I'm not going to let him go until you've come down here and made him answer some questions. I don't know what's been going on, but I'm not the fool you think me. This thing is going to be settled this morning, while I've got the old fellow here where I can see him."

"What old fellow?"

"This old butler, Biscoe. I— What the devil are you laughing at?"

"Is he there in the office?"

"Yes, I've told you. And he's staying here until—"

"Ask him," said Julian, "if the address Number 13 Abbess Avenue means anything to him. Go on, ask him and tell me what he says."

"Is this what you were finding out when you went off the other day?"

"I was. Go on, ask him."

"All right. Hold on. He says," reported Oliver after a few moments, "that he does know the address."

"I thought he would. What's he doing in the office in the first place?"

"He brought in a picture, a Clauval. At least, he says it's a Clauval. I haven't looked at it; it's wrapped up and it's addressed to you."

"To me?" The lightness had suddenly left Julian's manner.

"To you. There's a note."

A cloud, a small, fleeting cloud passed across the sun of Julian's morning. A note. A note . . .

"I'll come down," he said.

"You'd better."

200

He drove to the office, parked his car in a side street and walked round the corner, passing Mr. Stevens' shop and finding it impossible to believe that only a few days had passed since he had stood inside it, opening his heart to his friend Peke and making up his mind to go in search of a clue to Alexandra's whereabouts; only a few days since he had been in a fog of bewilderment and unhappiness. He had gone and he had returned and now it was all right. It was. It must be, it would be all right. There was only this note . . .

He ignored the gleaming new lift and took the stairs in energetic bounds. He pushed open the door of the outer office and stood for a moment glancing round him. In a corner —with an office boy, obviously on guard, beside him—sat Biscoe. Julian looked across at him, and the old man rose and gave him a timid smile. Julian was about to go over and talk to him when the door of Oliver's room opened and Oliver came out.

"One moment," he said.

Julian followed him into the room and Oliver shut the door.

"If you'll sit down," he said, "I'll ask you some of the things I've been turning over in my mind."

"Anything," said Julian. "But first, I want to see that picture and that note."

"They're on Father's desk," said Oliver. "I meant what I said, you know. I've known for some time that something's been up. These Clauvals have something to do with Mr. Randall, and before you leave the office, I'm—oh, here's Father."

He rose as Mr. Hurst came into the room and wished his sons good morning.

"Julian, there appears to be a package for you on my desk," he said. "Will you tell me what it's doing there?"

"I'm just going to look at it, sir," said Julian. "I'll be back in a moment."

He went out, crossed the office with a reassuring wave in Biscoe's direction, and went into his father's room. The package lay on the desk; Julian, with a brief look of apology towards the stenographer's back, walked to the desk and picked up the piece of paper on which, he felt, his future hopes depended. He looked at it: *Mr. Julian Hurst*—and, in one corner, written in neat capitals, *J.H. From A.B.*

From A.B. From . . .

Julian stared at the paper. It seemed to be moving. Watching with a sort of detached curiosity, he saw that his hands were trembling. His ears were full of sound and his heart was thumping. His eyes were on the paper, but now they were not seeing it; they were seeing something else—something he had seen, without seeing, as he entered the room. A neat back . . . a neat pair of ears, cocked at a listening angle . . . dark hair and . . .

He swung round, staring. Her head turned and a pair of blue eyes met his. She stood up and they remained for a moment face to face. There was no sound; she was waiting for him to speak and Julian was fighting for breath.

"Why, you—you—" he managed at last. "Why, you—"

"Good morning, Mr. Hurst," said Miss Bell.

"You—you—" Julian's voice ended in a croak. He advanced slowly towards her, his face dark with rage. "All these months, you—why, you—"

"I can explain everything, Mr. Hurst," said Alexandra tranquilly. "I can— Stay where you are!" she warned. "If you come a step nearer, I'll scream for—"

"A step nearer! Why, I'm going to break your ruddy little neck," promised Julian, between his teeth. "I'm going to— No!" His voice was suddenly panic-stricken. "No, Alexandra, no—*please!* For God's *sake*—"

It was no use. It was too late. Miss Bell, shutting her eyes tightly and opening her lovely mouth wide, had screamed loudly for assistance.

Chapter 14

"IN MY OWN OFFICE!" moaned Mr. Hurst, to his wife in the privacy of his study. "In my own office, before all those young boys and all those clerks, and all those young women! My own office, my own stenographer. My own son," he added, as an afterthought.

"It's all right, Edwin," said his wife soothingly, drawing up a chair and sitting down in an attempt to bring him comfort. "It's all right. They all understood it, you know."

"Understood it? How can anybody understand it? No doubt the story is being told in all their homes tonight—and with relish. The son of the head of the firm, and—"

"But she's such a *nice* girl, Edwin! Think of poor Julian looking for her everywhere, and not dreaming—"

"I don't understand it," said Mr. Hurst. "My head goes round trying to understand it. Everybody tells a different story; none of them agree. Why did Julian tell his aunt that the girl he had met was a cook?"

"She *was* a cook when he met her."

"She was nothing of the kind, my dear, and you know it. She was my stenographer and she had taken leave of absence, at a time when I could ill spare her, to go away and—she said—look after a sick relative. Where was the cooking in that?"

"But she was Mr. Randall's cook, Edwin."

"My dear, I've explained to you—she was his *granddaughter*."

"Yes, Edwin, but—"

"I don't understand it. It isn't at all the kind of courtship I can understand. A son of mine—"

"But you *like* her, Edwin, don't you?"

"I have nothing against her; she seems to me to be a nice-looking and a well-behaved young girl. Or she did until to-day. As a stenographer, as I've told you again and again, dear old Miss Sterndale understood what was wanted far, far better than—"

"After twenty years I dare say Alexandra would have been just as good."

"After twenty years I should not have been very much interested in how good a stenographer she was. Now I shall be expected to go through the routine of training a new girl, and I really can't face it. I shall do what I've been meaning to do, what I told Oliver I meant to do, I shall retire."

"But Oliver says that all the older clients would miss you so much. He needs you, Edwin."

"Things will be very well in his hands."

There was silence, and then Mrs. Hurst spoke in a thoughtful tone.

"Edwin, doesn't it seem wicked that all that money of

Mr. Randall's has to go to that society? Why shouldn't his granddaughter have some of it?"

"It's too late to go into that, my dear. Mr. Randall knew he had a granddaughter and he chose to leave her nothing. If I had known, if I had suspected—but we can't do anything now."

"But can't you? I mean, why can't you, as it were, divert something? There was so much! Couldn't just a few thousand pounds be given to Alexandra, to make up to her for all those years she had to work so hard?"

Mr. Hurst seemed to have some difficulty with his breathing.

"Do I understand you to say—" His voice was faint. "Are you actually suggesting to me, Mr. Randall's executor, that I should, as you put it, divert—"

"I'm sorry, Edwin. I was only *asking!* It just seemed to me so wicked, that's all, that an old man should be able to be so—"

Mr. Hurst sat up straighter in his chair and cleared his throat.

"Let me say a few words," he said gravely. "The word *trustee,* my dear, explains itself. The dictionary meaning is: one to whom something is entrusted. Entrusted. I am Mr. Randall's—"

"Yes, dear," said Mrs. Hurst, composing herself for a long session. "Yes?"

"Could I help it," asked Alexandra, "if you were stupid? Could I?"

They had the drawing room to themselves, and Julian was dividing the time equally between filling up gaps in his knowledge and making up for all the long months without sight or sound of her.

"You could have let me know when your grandfather died. You could have written—wired—phoned."

"What good would that have done?" enquired Alexandra.

"I would have come at once."

"You would have claimed the pictures."

"Why sell them yourself? Why not—"

"Those pictures," said Alexandra, "were all I had in the world."

"All?"

"All. I'd had a prospective husband for a few days, but he'd skipped off and—"

"When you first went to Father's office, did you have any idea that the firm acted for Mr. Randall?"

"None whatsoever," said Alexandra. "Even the Randall files didn't really make me connect the name with anybody belonging to me. There are lots of Randalls. It wasn't until I had to deal with the letter about the pictures that I knew, and it wasn't until I heard your father and your brother talking about the Clauvals that I understood which pictures they would turn out to be—if my grandfather still had them. I knew that they were the four pictures my mother had always talked about, and that I'd always longed to see. She never regretted anything else she left in her old home, but she could never, never understand why they had left the pictures behind, and she always longed to have them. So when I heard your father talking about them, I wondered how I could manage to get up there, to be there in case you found anything. And so I wrote to Biscoe. I hadn't seen him for years, but I knew he'd do anything I asked him to—anything honest. I told him I needed a holiday, but that I wanted to go on earning money while I was having it, and I suggested coming up to take the cook's place for a fortnight. So he arranged it, and there I was—and there you were."

"But why not *tell* me—"

"I didn't want to tell you anything about myself or about the pictures while I was at Holside. I felt that the wisest thing was to wait—I thought that I ought to leave you to find the Clauvals, if they were there; then I planned to meet you in London and ask you to see your father or your brother about them. Between us, I thought, we could think of some way in which I could have the pictures."

"But if you were going to meet me in London, Alexandra, then why, why, *why* did you send me to Nunn Road?"

Alexandra hesitated. Then she put up her hands and held them gently against Julian's ears.

"Perhaps you'd better not hear why," she said.

Julian caught her wrists and held them.

"All right, I won't listen," he said. "Now tell me. Why did you have to take the Clauvals from me and send me all round London trying to find you?"

"I didn't take the pictures from you," said Alexandra slowly, "until you—until I knew quite definitely that you had decided to go up to Scotland. You see, you gave a life-like imitation of a man who was feeling he'd acted too impulsively. You wanted time to think, and how did I know what you would think, up there far, far away from me? If you took the pictures with you, and—and never came back—"

"Darling, I—"

Alexandra took her hands from his ears and gently cupped his cheeks between them.

"Haven't you ever read about girls who are wooed by handsome strangers who leave them and never return? I had to be *sure*, Julian, don't you see? And so I took the pictures, and I made sure that you couldn't trace them and take them away from me—"

"But you could have—"

"And *then*," said Alexandra, "the whole position changed. My grandfather died, and I realized something that I'd never realized before—that Biscoe was going to have nothing to live on except a miserable old-age pension and the few pounds he'd been able to save."

"I could have seen to that, couldn't I?"

"Perhaps, but how did I know that you would ever come back?"

"Alexandra, I—"

"I'm not *blaming* you; I'm only trying to make you see the thing from my point of view. The important thing, suddenly, was Biscoe. I couldn't leave him to finish off his life on a miserable—"

"Why couldn't you have let me buy the pictures and donate the proceeds to Biscoe, as you wanted to do, without all that long separation?"

"It seemed to me that I hadn't any legal right to the pictures, and that if you helped me to sell them, you'd be an accessory after the fact. Have I worked in a lawyer's office for nothing?"

"All right. Go on."

"The way I decided to do it seemed the only way in which I could cover everything. I had the pictures; I could sell them and keep the money as a sort of fund for Biscoe; I could sell the pictures in places, or to people, who'd be sure to bring them to your notice. If you loved me, you'd buy them and keep them—for me. You did buy them."

"For myself."

"And so, you see, everything worked out all right, and if you hadn't been terribly, terribly mentally retarded, you would have been able to work it all out with no trouble."

"How did you know I wouldn't tell my father about the pictures?"

"I wasn't afraid of *that*. In fact, I was fairly safe all the way along. I knew you never went to the office; I knew that your brother wasn't the type who discussed office affairs, and particularly office stenographers, after office hours. Your father, when he spoke of his stenographer, meant the late lamented Miss Sterndale. It was quite safe to go into the shop and talk to your aunt; it was quite safe to go to Mr. Stevens' shop. There was a risk in going to your house, in case they'd heard my name, so I sent Biscoe, who thought it was all fair and aboveboard."

"But I might have mentioned your name at any time to Oliver."

"You might," agreed Alexander, "but I didn't see how you could talk your way out of having lost the pictures that Mr. Randall put into your charge, and so I didn't think it likely that you'd tell the story. I worried a bit in case you talked to your aunt, but even if you did tell her, I didn't think she'd know my name. But I felt safest of all because—"

"Because—?"

"Because I was keeping the fourth picture as a—as a safeguard. If you *were* so incredibly stupid that you didn't know who or where I was, then, at last, when I couldn't bear it any longer, I could use the fourth picture to bring you to me. And it did, you see?"

"Darling, I— Alexandra, can you ever—"

"Can I come in?" said a voice at the door. "No, I see I can't," went on Rowena.

"You're in," said Julian, "so you may as well stay in."

"Thank you. I always think a warm welcome is so heartening. You've had Alexandra in here for nearly two hours, and we're all pretty tired of waiting for you to realize that we all want to see her."

"Well, we've got a lot to talk about," said Julian. "There's a lot to arrange. We're going to be married as soon as people give us a chance to fix up the details."

"Are you really going to marry him, Alexandra?" asked Rowena.

"Yes, I am, I think," said Alexandra. "He isn't what I hoped for, but I've always heard that a clever girl can mould a man."

"My God!" said Julian. "Mould a man!"

"The only thing that's worrying me," said Alexandra, "is the difficulty of providing myself with a trousseau worthy of a setting more exalted than that of Pimlico."

"I can take a hint," said Rowena.

"You're very kind," said Alexandra, "because a girl can't very well let her fiancé pay for her trousseau, so—"

"Wait for it," Julian warned his aunt.

"—so what I decided to do," said Alexandra, "was to buy everything and let the bills stand over until after the wedding. Nobody can say that a man shouldn't pay for his wife's clothes."

"Where did you find this girl?" demanded Rowena. "You know, Alexandra," she went on, slowly, "I think—I'm not entirely sure—but I *think* that Julian has got all he deserves."

"I think so, too," said Alexandra.

Chapter 15

THE WEDDING was meant by the bride and bridegroom to be a rather quiet affair; they wanted it to be a gathering restricted to the family and their closest friends and this, in fact, it was. But the family, so scant on the bride's side, was revealed, on the bridegroom's, to be a very spreading affair; Campden Hill, Alexandra learned with awe, was but the London branch; there were, besides, the Kent branch and the Cambridgeshire branch, the Hertfordshire and Surrey branches, the unpopular Cumberland branch and the impoverished Hurst-Hursts from Rutland; lastly, there was Mr. St. John Hurst of Essex, said by his daughters to be the Head of the Family.

Friends on the bridegroom's side took up a mere half-pew —besides Mr. Peke Stevens, who acted as best man, there was but a sprinkling of chosen allies from schooldays. The bride, on the other hand, was responsible for assembling what her husband, looking over them wonderingly, pronounced to be the most heterogeneous collection of people he had ever seen outside a circus. Her explanation was that she had lived a life of toil; these were her fellow-toilers, and it would do him good to meet people who did something more arduous for their living than buying pictures from one person and selling them to another.

The two happiest people at the wedding, perhaps, were Mr. Hurst and Biscoe. Mr. Hurst, standing where he had been told to stand, shaking hands with innumerable people he had never met before and had no interest in meeting again, wore nevertheless a smile of great contentment. From time to time, he looked with placid satisfaction at a grey-haired woman in sober black, with sensible shoes—Miss Sterndale, who had agreed to come back to him and work at the new office for the year or two he had decided to remain with the firm. The new office with Miss Sterndale would be a very different place; going there each morning would be a pleasure, something he would look forward to without shrinking. He felt, and almost looked, a new man.

Biscoe was also full of quiet happiness. He was restored to his old dignity; though too deaf to announce guests who were unknown to him, he looked out for those whom he recognized, and gave himself the pleasure of introducing them to the company. He was to serve his old master's grand-daughter; Alexandra had told Julian that she would, if he wished, perform every other household office herself, but a butler she was going to have, and the butler was to be Biscoe.

There was a latecomer to the feast. A taxi drew up just after the speeches had been made and the bridal couple toasted. The passenger alighted, dropped her purse and tripped over the pavement's edge as she was stooping to recover it. She was steadied, and her property returned to her, by a policeman, a passer-by and two A A men. She then made her way towards the sounds of revelry; Biscoe saw her coming, and it was clear that he had no need to ask her name.

He threw the door open and waited for silence; then in a quavering but proud voice announced the last guest.

"Miss Doofer," he said.